Monsters & Demigods

by Tim Krause

A 5E COMPATIBLE REFERENCE

*Monsters, demons and demigods are the cornerstone to the most legendary adventures. Herein we've curated dozens and dozens of the most fearsome. Use them in skin-crawling crypts and at death-defying heights. Terrorize your party with demigods that will haunt them in their waking hours—if they survive the deadliest and most creative attacks! Full-color illustration, complete statistics and back-stories will help you, the Dungeon Master, **make your adventures truly memorable.***

This product created under the WOTC OGL, found in full at:
http://media.wizards.com/2016/downloads/SRD-OGL_V1.pdf

Images and maps are not covered under the WOTC OGL and are copyright 2019, Tomorrow River Games.

TOMORROW
RIVER GAMES

The author may be contacted at tgkrause@tomorrowrivergames.com
Support will be provided by
Tomorrow River Games (http://www.tomorrowrivergames.com)

TABLE OF CONTENTS

DEDICATION 4

CONTRIBUTORS 4

THE CREATURES 5

    ABHARTACH 5

    ARCH MAGE BREDON 6

    ASSASSIN (ARSÂMA) 7

    ASSASSIN (KORAG) 8

    BADGER 9

    BAN SITH 10

    BEAST OF BREY ROAD 11

    BELSNICKEL 12

    BON SECOUR 13

    BULETTE 14

    CATOBLEPAS 15

    CHIROGON 16

    CHOGAN (CROW) 17

    CHOZECH 18

    DARTFORD DEMON 19

    DEMON 20

    DEMON, DOG 21

    DEMON, VIMAK 22

    DARKSTONE DWARVES 23

    EAGLE, PLATINUM 24

    EFREETI 25

    EARTH ELEMENTAL 26

    FRAU PERCHTA 27

    GHOST, GRACELAND 28

    GHOST, HEADLESS 29

    GHOST, RIDGEWAY 30

    GRUAGACH 31

    GRÝLA 32

    HANS TRAPP 33

    HAUNCHIES OF MUSKEGO 34

    HODAG 35

    JÒLAKÖTTURINN 36

    KRAKE 37

    KRAMPUS 38

    LAKE MONSTER, PEPIE 39

    LAKE WINNEBAGO MONSTER 40

    LICH (KERAPTIS) 41

    MAKWA (BEAR) 42

    MASHENOMAK 43

    MINOTAUR 44

    MISAKAKOJISH (BADGER) 45

    MORRIGAN (ELVEN ARCHER) 46

    PÈRE FOUETTARD 47

QUESPER – CLERIC 48
QUESPER – MAGE 49
QUESPER – WARRIOR 50
ROGUE 51
THRAKOS 52
TÔLBANAKI - PRIEST 53
TÔLBANAKI - WARRIOR 54
VANCE, LORD AND LADY 55
UNDEAD (VATHRIS) 56
WIISAGI-MA (COYOTE) 57
WITCH (QUESPA) 58
YULE LADS 59
ZIIGWAN-MISKWA (STAG) 60
ZORMANTH 61

APPENDICES: NONPLAYER CHARACTERS **62**

ABENA (PALADIN) 62
ADENA (FIGHTER) 63
ANDER (FIGHTER) 64
BERNA (CLERIC) 65
CASTOR (WIZARD) 66
CHIEF WAPUKA (DRUID) 67
ERLON (PALADIN) 68
GORGO (WIZARD) 69
KURA (BARBARIAN) 70
RENÉ MENARD (CLERIC) 71
TELCHUR (WIZARD) 72
VELNIUS (RANGER) 73

APPENDICES: MORRIGAN'S LODGE OF LEGENDARY HUNTS **74**

APPENDICES: MISAKAKOJIS'S DEADLY WARREN **79**

APPENDICES: CREATURES BY TYPE **80**

APPENDICES: CREATURES BY CHALLENGE **81**

APPENDICES: CREATURES BY TERRAIN **82**

APPENDIX: MAGIC ITEMS OF LEGENDARIA **83**

APPENDIX: LEGENDARIA **84**

OPEN GAME LICENSE VERSION 1.0A **85**

KICKSTARTER SUPPORTERS **86**

MONSTER SKETCH BOOK **87**

DEDICATION

I've been writing and designing 5E compatible modules for a little over a year now, and it's been nothing short of a pleasure. I enjoy all of the process and am active in nearly every aspect of the process from concept to final production and distribution. But one of the aspects of game design that I am *not good at*: monster illustration.

This dedication is for all of the illustrators that I have had the pleasure of working with this year. Some of them are very familiar with the style I have been looking for, and others quite willing to learn and adapt. As I collected everything for this reference book, I was particularly struck by the sheer global nature of their backgrounds, and so listed their country of origin as part of the credits in the **contributor** section below. Truly, this is one of the most collaborative efforts that **Tomorrow River Games** has produced to date, and we look forward to many more.

Link arms, into the sunrise we march, adventurers all. And in the dead of night, we write on.

Tim, 29 November 2019

CONTRIBUTORS

Author	Tim Krause	
Cover Art	Alexy Beznutrov, Natalia Matuszewska	
Cover Layout	Tim Krause	
Illustration	Xavier Amiot	France
	Alexy Beznutrov	Russian Federation
	Sang Blat	Indonesia
	Design.bb	Serbia
	D.-experts360	Canada
	Paulo Duelli	Argentina
	Lezette Goosen	United Kingdom
	Natalia Matuszewska	United Kingdom
	Cornel Robisnon	Australia
	Cody Rostron	USA
	Senja	Bosnia
	Katia Tabakova	Bulgaria
	Zony Z.	Bangladesh

Naming Contributors		**Creature**		
	John Bowlin	Dwarves, Darkstone	Richard Sorden	Zormanth
	Jangus C. Cooper	Chogan	Frank Tilley	Nyzani
		Versteinern	Jessa	Tolbanaki
	Mark Featherstone	Bitter Thorn		
	Donna Krause	Bon Secour		
	Greg Krause	Kraku		
	Tami Mathison	Morrigan		
	Samantha Michaels	Kasula Faeyra		
	Robert Sabatke, Jr.	Chozech		
	Yordi Schaeken	Quesper		

ISBN: 9781712590096
First Printing: December 2019

THE CREATURES

Abhartach

An ancient evil, Abhartach will be found in only the deepest depths of the earth and is not your typical Vampire. This undead creature can survive for years, even centuries, without the blood of others. It will rely on a combination of stealth and attack to isolate its prey, attack and disappear without a trace. Destroying an Abhartach is truly the stuff of legends.

ABHARTACH
Medium undead (vampire), Lawful Evil

Armor Class 16 (natural armor)
Hit Points 144 (17d8+68)
Speed 30 ft.

STR	DEX	CON	INT	WIS	CHA
18 (+4)	18 (+4)	18 (+4)	17 (+3)	15 (+2)	18 (+4)

Saving Throws Dex +9, Wis +7, Cha +9
Skills Perception +7, Stealth +9
Damage Resistances bludgeoning, necrotic; bludgeoning, piercing, and slashing from nonmagical attacks
Condition Immunities charmed, frightened
Senses darkvision 120 ft., passive Perception 17
Languages Languages known in life
Challenge 13 (10,000 XP)

Shapechanger. Can polymorph into a bat or cloud of mist. Walking speed of 5'; flying of 30'.

Legendary Resistance (3/day). Can turn a failing save into success.

Misty Escape. At 0 HP, transforms into a cloud of mist. It must reach its resting place in 2 hours or be destroyed.

Regeneration. Regains 20 HP at the start of turn with at least 1 HP. Does not function if damage is from holy water or radiant damage.

Spider Climb. Can climb difficult surfaces without ability check.

Vampire Weaknesses. Forbiddance: Can't enter a home without permission.

Harmed by running water: 20 acid damage if it ends its turn in running water.

Stake to the heart: Paralyzed until the stake is removed.

Sunlight: 20 radiant damage if it starts its turn in sunlight. Disadvantage on attack and ability checks.

ACTIONS

Multiattack (vampire form only). Two attacks, only one of which can be a bite.

Unarmed Strike (vampire form only):. +9 to hit Melee, 5' reach; Hit: 8 (1d8+4) bludgeoning or grapple instead (DC 18 to escape).

Bite (vampire form only). +9 to hit, 5' reach; Hit: 7 (1d6+4) piercing plus 10 (3d6) necrotic damage. Target's maximum HP is reduced by necrotic damage taken and vampire regains same number of HP. Reduction lasts until target takes long rest. Target dies if maximum HP is reduced to 0.

Charm. Targets a victim within 30'. Target must save DC 17 Wisdom or be charmed. Vampire becomes a trusted friend. Effect lasts 24 hours.

Children of the Night (1/day). Magically calls 2d4 swarms of bats or 3d6 wolves. They will appear in 1d4 turns.

LEGENDARY ACTIONS

3 Legendary actions. Move: Move up to speed without provoking an attack of opportunity. Unarmed strike: makes one unarmed strike. Bite (2 actions): makes one bite attack. Can only make after end of another creature's turn.

Arch Mage Bredon

Many centuries ago, **Bredon** discovered what he believes to be the secret to immortality. He is an extremely intelligent spell caster, though he is also very safe when he attacks. At any thought of defeat, he will teleport away to a hidden chamber. All of his treasure is hidden in that lair.

ARCH MAGE (BREDON)

Medium humanoid (any race), any alignment

Armor Class 12 (15 with *mage armor*)
Hit Points 99 (18d8 + 18)
Speed 30 ft.

STR	DEX	CON	INT	WIS	CHA
10 (+0)	14 (+2)	12 (+1)	20 (+5)	15 (+2)	16 (+3)

Saving Throws Int +9, Wis +6
Skills Arcana +13, History +13
Damage Resistances damage from spells; non magical bludgeoning, piercing, and slashing (from stoneskin)
Senses passive Perception 12
Languages any six languages
Challenge 12 (8,400 XP)

Magic Resistance. The archmage has advantage on saving throws against spells and other magical effects.

Spellcasting. The archmage is an 18th-level spellcaster. Its spellcasting ability is Intelligence (spell save DC 17, +9 to hit with spell attacks). The archmage can cast disguise self and invisibility at will and has the following wizard spells prepared:

Cantrips (at will): *fire bolt, light, mage hand, prestidigitation, shocking grasp*
1st level (4 slots): *detect magic, identify, mage armor*, magic missile*
2nd level (3 slots): *detect thoughts, mirror image, misty step*
3rd level (3 slots): *counterspell, fly, lightning bolt*
4th level (3 slots): *banishment, fire shield, stoneskin**
5th level (3 slots): *cone of cold, scrying, wall of force*
6th level (1 slot): *globe of invulnerability*
7th level (1 slot): *teleport*
8th level (1 slot): *mind blank**
9th level (1 slot): *time stop*
* The archmage casts these spells on itself before combat.

ACTIONS

Dagger. *Melee or Ranged Weapon Attack:* +6 to hit, reach 5 ft. or range 20/60 ft., one target. *Hit:* 4 (1d4 + 2) piercing damage.

Assassin (Arsâma)

The looks of the best assassins can be deceiving, and his is no exception. **Arsâma** will attempt to join the party as an NPC and will only attack when he expects to kill his target. In the likeliest of scenarios, he will then flee. However, if Arsâma can cover for the attack and remain in the party he will do so.

ASSASSIN (ARSÂMA)
Medium humanoid (any race), any non-good alignment

Armor Class 16 (studded leather)
Hit Points 90 (12d8 + 36)
Speed 30 ft.

STR	DEX	CON	INT	WIS	CHA
11 (+0)	18 (+4)	16 (+3)	13 (+1)	12 (+1)	12 (+1)

Saving Throws Dex +7, Int +4
Skills Acrobatics +7, Deception +4, Perception +4, Stealth +10
Damage Resistances poison
Senses passive Perception 14
Languages Thieves' cant plus any two languages
Challenge 8 (3,900 XP)

Assassinate. During its first turn, the assassin has advantage on attack rolls against any creature that hasn't taken a turn. Any hit the assassin scores against a surprised creature is a critical hit.

Evasion. If the assassin is subjected to an effect that allows it to make a Dexterity saving throw to take only half damage, the assassin instead takes no damage if it succeeds on the saving throw, and only half damage if it fails.

Sneak Attack (1/Turn). The assassin deals an extra 13 (4d6) damage when it hits a target with a weapon attack and has advantage on the attack roll, or when the target is within 5 ft. of an ally of the assassin that isn't incapacitated and the assassin doesn't have disadvantage on the attack roll.

ACTIONS

Multiattack. The assassin makes two shortsword attacks.

Shortsword. *Melee Weapon Attack:* +6 to hit, reach 5 ft., one target. *Hit:* 6 (1d6 + 3) piercing damage, and the target must make a DC 15 Constitution saving throw, taking 24 (7d6) poison damage on a failed save, or half as much damage on a successful one.

Light Crossbow. *Ranged Weapon Attack:* +6 to hit, range 80/320 ft., one target. *Hit:* 7 (1d8 + 3) piercing damage, and the target must make a DC 15 Constitution saving throw, taking 24 (7d6) poison damage on a failed save, or half as much damage on a successful one.

Assassin (Korag)

Very little is known of **Korag**—one of the reputedly most elusive and dangerous of assassins.

ASSASSIN

Medium humanoid (any race), any non-good alignment

Armor Class 15 (studded leather)
Hit Points 78 (12d8 + 24)
Speed 30 ft.

STR	DEX	CON	INT	WIS	CHA
11 (+0)	16 (+3)	14 (+2)	13 (+1)	11 (+0)	10 (+0)

Saving Throws Dex +6, Int +4
Skills Acrobatics +6, Deception +3, Perception +3, Stealth +9
Damage Resistances poison
Senses passive Perception 13
Languages Thieves' cant plus any two languages
Challenge 8 (3,900 XP)

Assassinate. During its first turn, the assassin has advantage on attack rolls against any creature that hasn't taken a turn. Any hit the assassin scores against a surprised creature is a critical hit.

Evasion. If the assassin is subjected to an effect that allows it to make a Dexterity saving throw to take only half damage, the assassin instead takes no damage if it succeeds on the saving throw, and only half damage if it fails.

Sneak Attack (1/Turn). The assassin deals an extra 13 (4d6) damage when it hits a target with a weapon attack and has advantage on the attack roll, or when the target is within 5 ft. of an ally of the assassin that isn't incapacitated and the assassin doesn't have disadvantage on the attack roll.

ACTIONS

Multiattack. The assassin makes two shortsword attacks.

Shortsword. *Melee Weapon Attack:* +6 to hit, reach 5 ft., one target. *Hit:* 6 (1d6 + 3) piercing damage, and the target must make a DC 15 Constitution saving throw, taking 24 (7d6) poison damage on a failed save, or half as much damage on a successful one.

Light Crossbow. *Ranged Weapon Attack:* +6 to hit, range 80/320 ft., one target. *Hit:* 7 (1d8 + 3) piercing damage, and the target must make a DC 15 Constitution saving throw, taking 24 (7d6) poison damage on a failed save, or half as much damage on a successful one.

Badger

Badgers are a large, nocturnal creature. They will typically be a solitary encounter and will be most interested in defending their lairs. Lairs will have multiple tunnels and exits, though they will seldom be large than approximately 6-8 inches in diameter, making it difficult to pursue them once they retreat into their lairs.

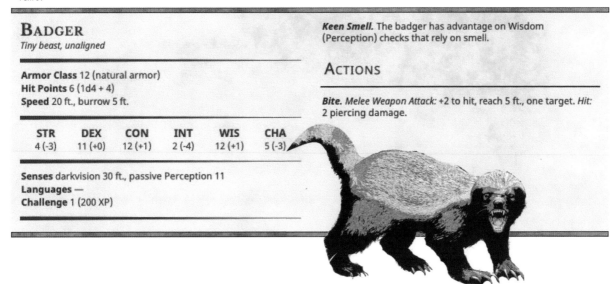

BADGER
Tiny beast, unaligned

Armor Class 12 (natural armor)
Hit Points 6 (1d4 + 4)
Speed 20 ft., burrow 5 ft.

STR	DEX	CON	INT	WIS	CHA
4 (-3)	11 (+0)	12 (+1)	2 (-4)	12 (+1)	5 (-3)

Senses darkvision 30 ft., passive Perception 11
Languages —
Challenge 1 (200 XP)

Keen Smell. The badger has advantage on Wisdom (Perception) checks that rely on smell.

ACTIONS

Bite. *Melee Weapon Attack:* +2 to hit, reach 5 ft., one target. *Hit:* 2 piercing damage.

Ban Sith

Ban Sith are usually tied to the place that they haunt by some prior trauma. They are also unlikely to leave those locations, and so seldom will pursue a retreating party.

BAN SITH
Medium undead (banshee), Chaotic Evil

Armor Class 12 (natural armor)
Hit Points 58 (13d8)
Speed 0 ft., fly 40 ft.

STR	DEX	CON	INT	WIS	CHA
1 (-5)	14 (+2)	10 (+0)	12 (+1)	11 (+0)	17 (+3)

Saving Throws Wis +2, Cha +5
Damage Resistances acid, fire, lightning, thunder; bludgeoning, piercing, and slashing from nonmagical attacks
Damage Immunities cold, necrotic, poison
Condition Immunities charmed, exhaustion, frightened, grappled, paralyzed, petrified, poisoned, prone, restrained
Senses darkvision 60 ft., passive Perception 10
Languages Common, Elvish
Challenge 4 (1,100 XP)

Detect Life. Can magically sense presence of living creatures up to 5 miles away (general location)

Incorporeal Movement. Can move through other creatures as difficult terrain. Takes 5 (1d10) damage if ends turn inside an object.

ACTIONS

Corrupting Touch. +4 to hit (spell attack), 5' reach; Hit: 12 (3d6+2) necrotic.

Horrifying Visage. Creatures within 60' that can see her must make DC 13 Wisdom save or be frightened for 1 minute. Can repeat at end of each turn with disadvantage.

Wail (1/day). Mournful wail within 30' must make DC 13 Constitution save or drop to 0 HP. On success, targets take 10 (3d6) psychic damage.

Beast of Brey Road

Something of legend, few believe the **Beast of Brey Road** even exists. It only attacks at dusk or evening and prefers moonless nights. It is a solitary beast, and will often be attacking near its lair, typically a cave or perhaps a very constrained canyon or cavern.

BEAST OF BREY ROAD
Medium humanoid (human), chaotic evil

Armor Class 11 in humanoid form, 12 (natural armor) in wolf or hybrid form
Hit Points 58 (9d8 + 18)
Speed 30 ft. (40 ft. in wolf form)

STR	DEX	CON	INT	WIS	CHA
15 (+2)	13 (+1)	14 (+2)	10 (+0)	11 (+0)	10 (+0)

Skills Perception +4
Damage Immunities bludgeoning, piercing, and slashing damage from nonmagical weapons that aren't silvered
Senses passive Perception 14
Languages Common (can't speak in wolf form)
Challenge 3 (700 XP)

Shapechanger. The beast can use its action to polymorph into a wolf-humanoid hybrid or into a wolf, or back into its true form, which is humanoid. Its statistics, other than its AC, are the same in each form. Any equipment it is wearing or carrying isn't transformed. It reverts to its true form if it dies.

Keen Hearing and Smell. The beast has advantage on Wisdom (Perception) checks that rely on hearing or smell.

ACTIONS

Multiattack (Humanoid or Hybrid Form Only). The beast of brey road makes two attacks: one with its bite and one with its claws or spear.

Bite (Beast or Hybrid Form Only). *Melee Weapon Attack:* +4 to hit, reach 5 ft., one target. *Hit:* 6 (1d8 + 2) piercing damage. If the target is a humanoid, it must succeed on a DC 12 Constitution saving throw or be cursed with werewolf lycanthropy.

Claws (Hybrid Form Only). *Melee Weapon Attack:* +4 to hit, reach 5 ft., one creature. *Hit:* 7 (2d4 + 2) slashing damage.

Spear (Humanoid Form Only). *Melee or Ranged Weapon Attack:* +4 to hit, reach 5 ft. or range 20/60 ft., one creature. *Hit:* 5 (1d6 + 2) piercing damage, or 6 (1d8 + 2) piercing damage if used with two hands to make a melee attack.

Belsnickel

Belsnickel appears as an elderly man who dresses in a patchwork of rags. If encountered on the streets, he will look no different than any other commoner.

BELSNICKEL
Huge giant, neutral good (50%) or neutral evil (50%)

Armor Class 14 (natural armor)
Hit Points 200 (16d12 + 96)
Speed 40 ft.

STR	DEX	CON	INT	WIS	CHA
27 (+8)	10 (+0)	22 (+6)	12 (+1)	16 (+3)	16 (+3)

Saving Throws Con +10, Wis +7, Cha +7
Skills Insight +7, Perception +7
Senses passive Perception 17
Languages Common, Giant
Challenge 9 (5,000 XP)

Keen Smell. The belsnickel has advantage on Wisdom (Perception) checks that rely on smell.

ACTIONS

Multiattack. The giant makes two whip attacks.

Whip. *Melee Weapon Attack:* +12 to hit, reach 10 ft., one target. *Hit:* 21 (3d8 + 8) piercing damage.

Bon Secour

The **Bon Secour** inhabits only the deepest of freshwater lakes and has been seldom seen. Fishermen tell tales of an enormous fish that has capsized their small crafts, though few survive such attacks. Bon Secour seeks to devour its prey.

BON SECOUR
Large giant, chaoticl evil

Armor Class 20 (natural armor)
Hit Points 130 (20d8 + 40)
Speed 0 ft., swim 50 ft.

STR	DEX	CON	INT	WIS	CHA
14 (+2)	14 (+2)	14 (+2)	20 (+5)	15 (+2)	13 (+1)

Saving Throws Dex +6, Int +9, Wis +6
Skills History +13, Perception +10, Stealth +6
Damage Immunities bludgeoning, piercing, and slashing from nonmagical attacks
Senses blindsight 30 ft., darkvision 120 ft., passive Perception 20
Languages telepathy 120 ft.
Challenge 11 (7,200 XP)

Probing Telepathy. If a creature communicates telepathically with the bon secour, the creature learns the creature's greatest desires if the creature can see the creature.

ACTIONS

Multiattack. The bon secour makes three fin or tail attacks.

Tail. *Melee Weapon Attack:* +9 to hit, reach 10 ft. one target. *Hit:* 15 (3d6 + 5) bludgeoning damage.

Enslave (3/day). The bon secour targets one creature it can see within 30 ft. of it. The target must succeed on a DC 14 Wisdom saving throw or be magically charmed by the bon secour until the bon secour dies or until it is on a different plane of existence from the target. The charmed target is under the bon secour's control and can't take reactions, and the bon secour and the target can communicate telepathically with each other over any distance.

Whenever the charmed target takes damage, the target can repeat the saving throw. On a success, the effect ends. No more than once every 24 hours, the target can also repeat the saving throw when it is at least 1 mile away from the bon secour.

Bite. *Melee Weapon Attack:* +9 to hit, reach 10 ft., one target. *Hit:* 12 (2d6 + 5) bludgeoning damage. If the target is a creature, it must succeed on a DC 14 Constitution saving throw or become diseased. The disease has no effect for 1 minute and can be removed by any magic that cures disease. After 1 minute, the diseased creature's skin becomes translucent and slimy, the creature can't regain hit points unless it is underwater, and the disease can be removed only by heal or another disease-curing spell of 6th level or higher. When the creature is outside a body of water, it takes 6 (1d12) acid damage every 10 minutes unless moisture is applied to the skin before 10 minutes have passed.

LEGENDARY ACTIONS

The Bon Secour can take 3 legendary actions, choosing from the options below. Only one legendary action option can be used at a time and only at the end of another creature's turn. The Bon Secour regains spent legendary actions at the start of its turn.

Detect. The bon secour makes a Wisdom (Perception) check.
Tail Swipe. The bon secour makes one tail attack.
Psychic Drain (Costs 2 Actions). One creature charmed by the bon secour takes 10 (3d6) psychic damage, and the bon secour regains hit points equal to the damage the creature takes.

Bulette

The **Bulette** is a solitary creature, particularly known for its ability to jump great distances (including vertical) even from a dead standstill.

BULETTE
Large monstrosity, unaligned

Armor Class 17 (natural armor)
Hit Points 94 (9d10 + 45)
Speed 40 ft., burrow 40 ft.

STR	DEX	CON	INT	WIS	CHA
19 (+4)	11 (+0)	21 (+5)	2 (-4)	10 (+0)	5 (-3)

Skills Perception +6
Senses darkvision 60 ft., tremorsense 60 ft., passive Perception 16
Languages —
Challenge 5 (1,800 XP)

Standing Leap. The bulette's long jump is up to 30 ft. and its high jump is up to 15 ft., with or without a running start.

ACTIONS

Bite. *Melee Weapon Attack:* +7 to hit, reach 5 ft., one target. *Hit:* 30 (4d12 + 4) piercing damage.

Deadly Leap. If the bulette jumps at least 15 ft. as part of its movement, it can then use this action to land on its ft. in a space that contains one or more other creatures. Each of those creatures must succeed on a DC 16 Strength or Dexterity saving throw (target's choice) or be knocked prone and take 14 (3d6 + 4) bludgeoning damage plus 14 (3d6 + 4) slashing damage. On a successful save, the creature takes only half the damage, isn't knocked prone, and is pushed 5 ft. out of the bulette's space into an unoccupied space of the creature's choice. If no unoccupied space is within range, the creature instead falls prone in the bulette's space.

Catoblepas

A weak neck betrays the true, horrific power of the **Catoblepas**. It has the head of a boar, and thick scaly skin. Because its neck is so weak, its head is often directed toward the ground. It is drawn toward the most rancid flora and is often found in and around swamps and fen.

CATOBLEPAS
Large monstrosity, unaligned

Armor Class 14 (natural armor)
Hit Points 84 (8d10+40)
Speed 30 ft.

STR	DEX	CON	INT	WIS	CHA
19 (+4)	12 (+1)	21 (+5)	3 (-4)	14 (+2)	8 (-1)

Senses darkvision 60 ft., passive Perception 12
Languages —
Challenge 5 (1,800 XP)

Downward Looking. Disadvantage on Perception checks

Intimidating. A Catoblepas has an appearance so grim and ugly that anyone within 10' must make DC 14 Wisdom save or, suffer disadvantage on melee attacks against the creature. A creature can repeat the saving throw at the end of each of its turns.

Resilient. If a Catoblepas takes 10 damage or less that would reduce it to 0 hit points, it is reduced to 1 hit point instead.

ACTIONS

Tusk Attack. Melee Weapon Attack: +7 to hit, reach 10 ft., one creature. Hit: 11 (2d6 + 4) piercing damage.

Poison Breath (Recharge 4-6). A Catoblepas exhales poisonous gas in a 15' cone. Creatures must make a DC 13 Constitution save, suffering 17 (5d6) poison damage on a failed save and half as much damage on a successful one.

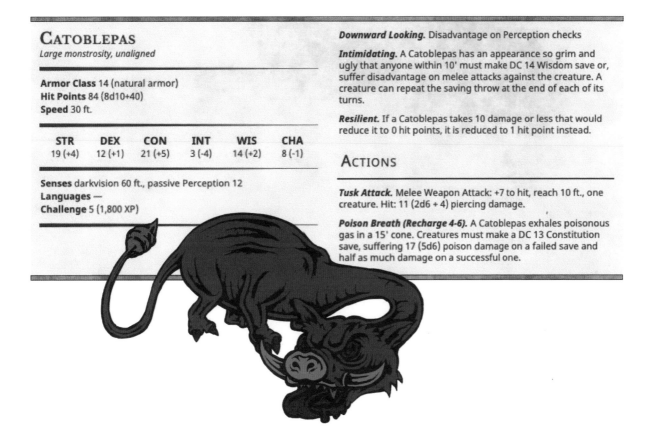

Chirogon

This large, flying humanoid is dangerous in that it cannot only attack multiple times, but has a dangerous acid breath weapon. Many believe that **Chirogon** is descended from a race of dragon people. It prefers to attack at night and will retreat if its HP are dropped below half.

CHIROGON
Large humanoid (chirogon), Chaotic

Armor Class 13 (natural armor)
Hit Points 72 (7d10+35)
Speed 40 ft., fly 60 ft. (hover)

STR	DEX	CON	INT	WIS	CHA
18 (+4)	16 (+3)	15 (+2)	6 (-2)	14 (+2)	20 (+5)

Saving Throws Str +7, Cha +8
Skills Perception +5, Stealth +6
Damage Immunities poison
Condition Immunities grappled, paralyzed, restrained
Senses blindsight 60 ft., darkvision 30 ft., passive Perception 15
Languages Common, Draconic
Challenge 7 (2,900 XP)

ACTIONS

Multiattack. 2 attacks: one bite, one claw.

Bite. +10, 5' reach; Hit: 9 (1d8+5)

Claw. +7, 5' reach; Hit: 7 (1d4+5)

Breath Weapon (Recharge: 5-6). 60' line of acid Hit: 21 (7d6); DC 18 or half damage on success.

Chogan (Crow)

Chogan is the wisest of the *Sapelo Deities*. She is able to summon large swarms (1d100+50) of **Krake** at will, and they will appear in 1d4 turns. They will fight to the death for Chogan, but because they are magical, their bodies disappear when their HP are reduced to 0. If it suits her, Chogan will come to the aid of the other *Sapelo Deities*.

CHOGAN (CROW)
Large fey (crow), Chaotic Neutral

Armor Class 17 (natural armor)
Hit Points 161 (17d10+68)
Speed 40 ft., fly 90 ft.

STR	DEX	CON	INT	WIS	CHA
17 (+3)	22 (+6)	19 (+4)	18 (+4)	22 (+6)	21 (+5)

Saving Throws Str +8, Wis +11, Cha +10
Skills Acrobatics +11, Athletics +8, History +9, Perception +11
Damage Resistances bludgeoning, cold; bludgeoning, piercing, and slashing from nonmagical attacks
Damage Immunities lightning, thunder
Condition Immunities charmed, frightened, grappled, incapacitated, poisoned, restrained, stunned
Senses truesight 120 ft., passive Perception 21
Languages All, telepathy 120 ft.
Challenge 14 (11,500 XP)

Passive Perception. 21

Bird Passivism. No bird can willingly attack crow.

Flyby. Doesn't provoke an opportunity attack when she flies out of enemy reach.

Magic Resistance. Advantage on saving throws against spells and other magic effects

Rejuvination. Reforms in 1d6 on asral plane

Shapechanger. Can use action to change into a platinum eagle, a medium, raven-haired human woman, or back into a crow. Statistics remain the same in each form.

Speak with Birds. Can communicate with birds

Innate Spellcasting. Charisma (Spell save DC 18, +10 to hit spell attacks); Can cast:
 At will: dispel magic, gust of wind, spiritual weapon
 3/day each: chain lightning, counterspell
 1/day: control weather

ACTIONS

Storm Strike Weapons. Weapon attacks are magical. Attack deals an extra 2d6 damage as either lightning or thunder (part of attack).

Multiattack. Two attacks in eagle or humanoid form; three attacks as crow: one talon, two spear

Storm Spear (Crow or Human only). +11 to Hit, melee or ranged; 5' reach. Hit: 13 (2d6+6) slashing plus 9 (2d8) lightning or thunder. Target is grappled (DC 18 escape). Can automatically hit with talons until grapple ends. Grappled targets move with her.

Talons (Eagle or True Form). +11 to hit, 5' reach. Hit: 11 (2d4+6) slashing plus 9 (2d8) lightning or thunder. Target is grappled (DC 18 escape). Can automatically hit with talons until grapple ends. Grappled targets move with her.

REACTIONS

Parry. Adds 5 to AC against one melee attack that would hit.

LEGENDARY ACTIONS

Can only be used at the end of another creature's turn. Regains at the start of her turn.

Legendary Resistance (2/day). Can choose to succeed on a failed savings throw.
Soar (Eagle or Crow). Flies up to her flying speed.
Storm Spear (Humanoid or Crow). Makes a storm spear attack.
Swooping Death (eagle or crow only). Costs 2 actions; Attacks with talons. If the attack hits, can fly up to half her flying speed.

Chozech

Chozech are legendary for their blood-curdling shrieks. These large monsters thrive in both fresh and saltwater. They will attack fishing and other small water vessels, focusing almost exclusively on pulling their prey into the water with them.

CHOZECH
Large monstrosity, Unaligned

Armor Class 13 (natural armor)
Hit Points 97 (13d10+26)
Speed 0 ft., swim 50 ft.

STR	DEX	CON	INT	WIS	CHA
16 (+3)	15 (+2)	15 (+2)	3 (-4)	12 (+1)	4 (-3)

Senses darkvision 60 ft., tremorsense 10 ft., passive Perception 11
Languages —
Challenge 4 (1,100 XP)

Camoflauge. The chozech has advantage on Dexterity (Stealth) checks when underwater.

Swallow. If the chozech bites a grappled target, it is swallowed and the grapple ends. Once swallowed, the target is blinded and restrained. Target takes 10 (3d6) acid damage start of the chozech's next turn. If the chozech dies, the target can use 5' of movement to crawl out of the corpse.

ACTIONS

Multiattack. The chozech uses its shriek, and makes two bite attacks.

Bite. +5 hit, 5' reach; Hit: 10 (2d6+3) piercing damage. Creature is grappled (escape DC 13 strength) until it escapes. The chozech can only bite grappled target (at advantage).

Shriek. The chozech lets out a blood-curdling shriek. Targets within 40' must save DC 12 Constitution or be frightened until the start of the chozech's next turn. Saves are immune from shrieks for next 24 hours.

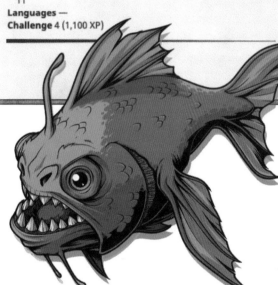

Name: Robert Sabatke, Jr.

Dartford Demon

The **Dartford Demon** is said to roam the local hills and forests. His bite and whip are legendary in the damage they inflict, though often only the scant remains of victims can be found. There have been few reportings of a very large, hairy man-like creature, though little other details are available about the Dartford Demon.

DARTFORD DEMON

Large fiend (devil), lawful evil

Armor Class 17 (natural armor)
Hit Points 168 (16d10 + 80)
Speed 40 ft.

STR	DEX	CON	INT	WIS	CHA
24 (+7)	17 (+3)	20 (+5)	11 (+0)	14 (+2)	19 (+4)

Saving Throws Str +11, Dex +7, Con +9, Wis +6, Cha +8
Skills Athletics +11, Intimidation +8
Damage Resistances cold; bludgeoning, piercing, and slashing from nonmagical weapons that aren't silvered
Damage Immunities fire, poison
Condition Immunities poisoned
Senses passive Perception 12
Languages Common, telepathy 100 ft.
Challenge 10 (5,900 XP)

Devil's Sight. Magical darkness doesn't impede the devil's darkvision.

Magic Resistance. The automata devil has advantage on saving throws against spells and other magical effects.

Innate Spellcasting. the automata devils' spellcasting ability is Charisma (spell save DC 16). It can innately cast the following spells, requiring no material components:

at will: *charm person, suggestion, teleport*
1/day each: *banishing smite, cloudkill*

ACTIONS

Multiattack. The automata devil makes two melee attacks, using any combination of bite, claw, and whip attacks. The bite attack can be used only once per turn.

Bite. *Melee Weapon Attack:* +11 to hit, reach 5 ft., one target. *Hit:* 18 (2d10 + 7) slashing damage.

Claw. *Melee Weapon Attack:* +11 to hit, reach 5 ft., one target. *Hit:* 14 (2d6 + 7) slashing damage.

Whip. *Melee Weapon Attack:* +11 to hit, reach 15 ft., one target. *Hit:* 11 (1d8 + 7) slashing damage and the target is grappled (escape DC 17) and restrained. Only two targets can be grappled by the automata devil at one time, and each grappled target prevents one whip from being used to attack. An individual target can be grappled by only one whip at a time. A grappled target takes 9 (2d8) piercing damage at the start of its turn.

Punishing Maw. If a target is already grappled in a whip at the start of the automata devil's turn, both creatures make opposed Strength (Athletics) checks. If the grappled creature wins, it takes 9 (2d8) piercing damage and remains grappled. If the devil wins, the grappled creature is dragged into the devil's stomach maw, a mass of churning gears, razor teeth, and whirling blades. The creature takes 49 (4d20 + 7) slashing damage and is grappled, and the whip is free to attack again on the devil's next turn. The creature takes another 49 (4d20 + 7) slashing damage automatically at the start of each of the automata devil's turns for as long as it remains grappled in the maw. Only one creature can be grappled in the punishing maw at a time. The automata devil can freely "spit out"a creature or corpse during its turn, to free up the maw for another victim.

Fear Aura. Automata devils radiate fear in a 10-foot radius. A creature that starts its turn in the affected area must make a successful DC 16 Wisdom saving throw or become frightened. A creature that makes the save successfully cannot be affected by the same automata devil's fear aura again.

Demon

DEMON
Large fiend (devil), lawful evil

Armor Class 14 (natural armor)
Hit Points 108 (10d10 + 85)
Speed 20 ft., fly 60 ft.

STR	DEX	CON	INT	WIS	CHA
18 (+4)	15 (+2)	18 (+4)	12 (+1)	16 (+3)	17 (+3)

Saving Throws Str +7, Dex +5, Wis +6, Cha +6
Damage Resistances cold; bludgeoning, piercing, and slashing from nonmagical weapons that aren't silvered
Damage Immunities fire, poison
Condition Immunities poisoned
Senses darkvision 120 ft., passive Perception 13
Languages Infernal, telepathy 120 ft.
Challenge 6 (2,300 XP)

Demon's Sight. Magical darkness doesn't impede the demon's darkvision.

ACTIONS

Multiattack. The demon makes three melee attacks: two with its fork. It can use Hurl Flame in place of any melee attack.

Fork. *Melee Weapon Attack:* +10 to hit, reach 10 ft., one target. *Hit:* 15 (2d8 + 6) piercing damage.

Hurl Flame. *Ranged Spell Attack:* +7 to hit, range 150 ft., one target. *Hit:* 14 (4d6) fire damage. If the target is a flammable object that isn't being worn or carried, it also catches fire.

Demon, Dog

The **Demon Dog** is nothing short of legend, supposedly hunting with **Morrigan**, the ghostly elven archer. It is both swift and deadly with its attacks giving rise to legends about having two heads – which has never been proven (and are untrue).

DEMON DOG
Medium monstrosity, neutral evil

Armor Class 12
Hit Points 39 (6d8 + 12)
Speed 40 ft.

STR	DEX	CON	INT	WIS	CHA
15 (+2)	14 (+2)	14 (+2)	3 (-4)	13 (+1)	6 (-2)

Skills Perception +5, Stealth +4
Senses darkvision 120 ft., passive Perception 15
Languages —
Challenge 1 (200 XP)

Two-Headed. The dog has advantage on Wisdom (Perception) checks and on saving throws against being blinded, charmed, deafened, frightened, stunned, or knocked unconscious.

ACTIONS

Multiattack. The dog makes two bite attacks.

Bite. *Melee Weapon Attack:* +4 to hit, reach 5 ft., one target. *Hit:* 5 (1d6 + 2) piercing damage. If the target is a creature, it must succeed on a DC 12 Constitution saving throw against disease or become poisoned until the disease is cured. Every 24 hours that elapse, the creature must repeat the saving throw, reducing its hit point maximum by 5 (1d10) on a failure. This reduction lasts until the disease is cured. The creature dies if the disease reduces its hit point maximum to 0.

Demon, Vimak

Depending on your adventure, treat **Vimak** as the demon that controls **Keraptis** (see Lich).

DEMON (VIMAK)
Large fiend (demon), chaotic evil

Armor Class 18 (natural armor)
Hit Points 189 (18d10 + 90)
Speed 40 ft.

STR	DEX	CON	INT	WIS	CHA
18 (+4)	20 (+5)	20 (+5)	18 (+4)	16 (+3)	20 (+5)

Saving Throws Str +9, Con +10, Wis +8, Cha +10
Damage Resistances cold, fire, lightning; bludgeoning, piercing, and slashing from nonmagical weapons
Damage Immunities poison
Condition Immunities poisoned
Senses truesight 120 ft., passive Perception 13
Languages Abyssal, telepathy 120 ft.
Challenge 16 (15,000 XP)

Magic Resistance. The demon (vimak) has advantage on saving throws against spells and other magical effects.

Magic Weapons. The demon (vimak)'s weapon attacks are magical.

Reactive. The demon (vimak) can take one reaction on every turn in combat.

ACTIONS

Multiattack. The demon (vimak) can make seven attacks: six with its longswords and one with its tail.

Longsword. *Melee Weapon Attack:* +9 to hit, reach 5 ft., one target. *Hit:* 13 (2d8 + 4) slashing damage.

Tail. *Melee Weapon Attack:* +9 to hit, reach 10 ft., one creature. *Hit:* 15 (2d10 + 4) bludgeoning damage. If the target is Medium or smaller, it is grappled (escape DC 19). Until this grapple ends, the target is restrained, the demon (vimak) can automatically hit the target with its tail, and the demon (vimak) can't make tail attacks against other targets.

Teleport. The demon (vimak) magically teleports, along with any equipment it is wearing or carrying, up to 120 feet to an unoccupied space it can see.

REACTIONS

Parry. The demon (vimak) adds 5 to its AC against one melee attack that would hit it. To do so, the demon (vimak) must see the attacker and be wielding a melee weapon.

Darkstone Dwarves

Darkstone dwarves average 2-6 inches shorter than regular dwarves. Their eyes are largely sightless and very small from generations of working in the mines. They are exceptionally strong and are able to endure the extremes of both heat and humidity.

Sometimes called the Bryglurs, there are only a handful of them in existence, descending from Bryglur Darkstone's clan—a group of surface dwarves that lived on the continent some 500 years ago. Bryglur Darkstone was a legendary hero of yore that helped broker a long-lasting era of peace and prosperity between dwarves, humans and elves.

Generations later, the Darkstone were driven from their homelands by a vicious hoard of humanoids led by the dark elf wizard Raazlekurghe. Most of the survivors sought refuge on Sapelo Island. Since they were descended from surface dwarves, their time spent underground has had a negative impact on their eyesight.

DARKSTONE DWARVES
Medium humanoid, chaotic neutral

Armor Class 12 (natural armor)
Hit Points 82 (11d6+44)
Speed 30 ft.

STR	DEX	CON	INT	WIS	CHA
20 (+5)	12 (+1)	18 (+4)	10 (+0)	10 (+0)	10 (+0)

Saving Throws Str +7, Con +6
Skills Intimidation +2, Perception +2, Survival +2
Senses darkvision 120 ft., passive Perception 12
Languages —
Challenge 4 (1,100 XP)

Evasive. Against attacks/effects that allow Dexterity saving throws for half damage, darkstone dwarves takes no damage, or half on a failed save.

Shadowstrike. Weapon attacks deal additional 9 (2d8) necrotic damage

ACTIONS

Multiattack. Makes two axe attacks

Axe. +7, 5' reach; Hit: 7 (1d6+4) slashing plus 9 (2d8) necrotic.

Darkness Insanity. Chooses a creature within 30' and assaults it with its mind. Must succeed on a DC 13 Wisdom save or be confused for 1 minute. Can repeat saving throw at the end of each turn.

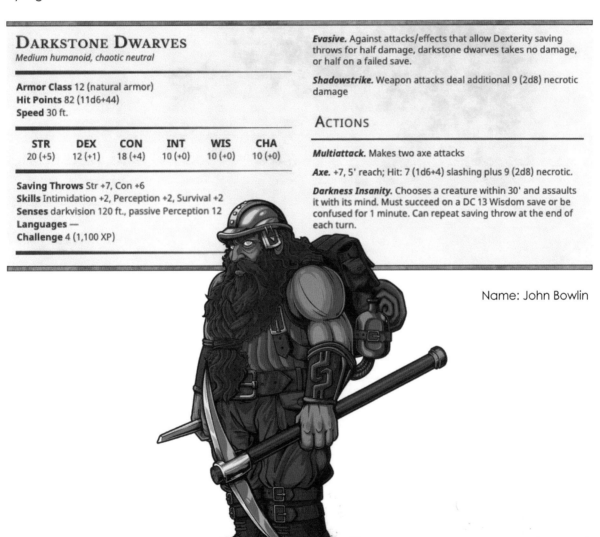

Name: John Bowlin

Eagle, Platinum

These majestic **eagles** are slightly larger than golden eagles. Their feathers are largely platinum, though their tail feathers are banded with gold. They are extremely uncommon but are known for their telepathic abilities.

EAGLE, PLATINUM
Medium celestial, neutral good

Armor Class 20 (natural armor)
Hit Points 99 (18d6+36)
Speed 20 ft., fly 120 ft.

STR	DEX	CON	INT	WIS	CHA
12 (+1)	19 (+4)	16 (+3)	18 (+4)	16 (+3)	20 (+5)

Saving Throws Dex +6, Int +6, Wis +5, Cha +7
Skills Acrobatics +6, Arcana +6, Insight +5, Medicine +5, Nature +6, Perception +5, Religion +6
Damage Immunities fire, lightning; bludgeoning, piercing, and slashing from nonmagical attacks
Condition Immunities charmed, frightened, invisible
Senses darkvision 60 ft., truesight 60 ft., passive Perception 15
Languages Common, Elvish
Challenge 4 (1,100 XP)

Innate Spellcasting. Charisma (spell save DC 15)

At will: guidance, purify food and drink, speak with animals

3/day each: charm person, cure wounds (2d8+5), daylight, tongues

1/day each: heal, reincarnate

ACTIONS

Multiattack. Makes one bite and two claw attacks.

Bite. +5, 5' reach; Hit: 8 (1d10 + 3) piercing, plus 3 (1d6) lightning damage.

Claw. +6, 5' reach; Hit: 10 (2d8+4), slashing.

Lightning Breath (Recharge 5-6). The eagle, platinum exhales lightning in a 30' line that is 5' wide. Each creature in that line must make a DC 12 Dexterity saving throw, taking 22 (4d10) lightning damage on a failed save, or half as much on a successful one.

Efreeti

EFREETI
Large elemental, lawful evil

Armor Class 17 (natural armor)
Hit Points 200 (16d10 + 112)
Speed 40 ft., fly 60 ft.

STR	DEX	CON	INT	WIS	CHA
22 (+6)	12 (+1)	24 (+7)	16 (+3)	15 (+2)	16 (+3)

Saving Throws Int +7, Wis +6, Cha +7
Damage Immunities fire
Senses darkvision 120 ft., passive Perception 12
Languages Ignan
Challenge 11 (7,200 XP)

Elemental Demise. If the efreeti dies, its body disintegrates in a flash of fire and puff of smoke, leaving behind only equipment the djinni was wearing or carrying.

Innate Spellcasting. The efreeti's innate spell casting ability is Charisma (spell save DC 15, +7 to hit with spell attacks). It can innately cast the following spells, requiring no material components:

At will: *detect magic*
3/day: *enlarge/reduce, tongues*
1/day each: *conjure elemental* (fire elemental only), *gaseous form, invisibility, major image, plane shift, wall of fire*

Variant: Genie Powers. Genies have a variety of magical capabilities, including spells. A few have even greater powers that allow them to alter their appearance or the nature of reality.

Disguises. Some genies can veil themselves in illusion to pass as other similarly shaped creatures. Such genies can innately cast the disguise self spell at will, often with a longer duration than is normal for that spell. Mightier genies can cast the true polymorph spell one to three times per day, possibly with a longer duration than normal. Such genies can change only their own shape, but a rare few can use the spell on other creatures and objects as well.

Wishes. The genie power to grant wishes is legendary among mortals. Only the most potent genies, such as those among the nobility, can do so. A particular genie that has this power can grant one to three wishes to a creature that isn't a genie. Once a genie has granted its limit of wishes, it can't grant wishes again for some amount of time (usually 1 year). and cosmic law dictates that the same genie can expend its limit of wishes on a specific creature only once in that creature's existence.

To be granted a wish, a creature within 60 feet of the genie states a desired effect to it. The genie can then cast the wish spell on the creature's behalf to bring about the effect. Depending on the genie's nature, the genie might try to pervert the intent of the wish by exploiting the wish's poor wording. The perversion of the wording is usually crafted to be to the genie's benefit.

ACTIONS

Multiattack. The efreeti makes two scimitar attacks or uses its Hurl Flame twice.

Scimitar. *Melee Weapon Attack:* +10 to hit, reach 5 ft., one target. *Hit:* 13 (2d6 + 6) slashing damage plus 7 (2d6) fire damage.

Hurl Flame. *Ranged Spell Attack:* +7 to hit, range 120 ft., one target. *Hit:* 17 (5d6) fire damage.

Earth Elemental

EARTH ELEMENTAL
Large elemental, neutral

Armor Class 17 (natural armor)
Hit Points 126 (12d10 + 60)
Speed 30 ft., burrow 30 ft.

STR	DEX	CON	INT	WIS	CHA
20 (+5)	8 (-1)	20 (+5)	5 (-3)	10 (+0)	5 (-3)

Damage Vulnerabilities thunder
Damage Resistances bludgeoning, piercing, and slashing from
nonmagical weapons
Damage Immunities poison
Condition Immunities exhaustion, paralyzed, petrified,
poisoned, unconscious
Senses darkvision 60 ft., tremorsense 60 ft., passive Perception
10
Languages Terran
Challenge 5 (1,800 XP)

Earth Glide. The elemental can burrow through nonmagical,
unworked earth and stone. While doing so, the elemental
doesn't disturb the material it moves through.

Siege Monster. The elemental deals double damage to objects
and structures.

ACTIONS

Multiattack. The elemental makes two slam attacks.

Slam. *Melee Weapon Attack:* +8 to hit, reach 10 ft., one target.
Hit: 14 (2d8 + 5) bludgeoning damage.

Frau Perchta

No one knows how long **Frau Perchta** witches have ruled the night. They are dangerous spellcasters who draw their power from the darkness of midnight.

FRAU PERCHTA
Medium fey (undead), chaotic evil

Armor Class 17 (natural armor)
Hit Points 91 (14d8 + 28)
Speed 30 ft.

STR	DEX	CON	INT	WIS	CHA
13 (+1)	16 (+3)	14 (+2)	12 (+1)	13 (+1)	16 (+3)

Saving Throws Wis +4
Skills Nature +4, Perception +4, Stealth +6, Survival +4
Damage Immunities cold
Condition Immunities charmed, frightened, paralyzed, poisoned
Senses darkvision 60 ft., passive Perception 14
Languages Auran, Common, Giant
Challenge 7 (2,900 XP)

Graystaff Magic. Carries a graystaff that serves as a broom of flying. Can cast additional spells, noted below. Only Frau Perchta may use the graystaff.

Spells:
Hold person
Ray of frost
Cone of cold (3/day)
Ice Storm (3/day)
Wall of Ice (3/day)
Control Weather (1/day)

ACTIONS

Slam. +4, 5' reach; Hit: 10 bludgeoning plus 3 cold

Maddening Feast. Feasts on the corpse of an enemy within 5'. Any creature watching, saves DC 15 Wisdom or frightened for 1 minute. May repeat save end of every turn.

Innate Spellcasting. Charisma, DC 14, +6 to hit

Ice Walk. Move across icy surfaces without ability checks. Difficult ice or snow terrain doesn't cost extra movement.

Ghost, Graceland

The **Graceland Ghost** is reputed to haunt a cemetery by the same name. Little is known about the ghost other than that most who claim to have seen it end up running in fear. While most do in fact run from fear, the ghost will attempt to possess any party members who are able to stay and fight.

GHOST, GRACELAND
Medium undead, any alignment

Armor Class 11
Hit Points 45 (10d8)
Speed 0 ft., fly 40 ft. (hover)

STR	DEX	CON	INT	WIS	CHA
7 (-2)	13 (+1)	10 (+0)	10 (+0)	12 (+1)	17 (+3)

Damage Resistances acid, fire, lightning, thunder; bludgeoning, piercing, and slashing from nonmagical weapons
Damage Immunities cold, necrotic, poison
Condition Immunities charmed, exhaustion, frightened, grappled, paralyzed, petrified, poisoned, prone, restrained
Senses darkvision 60 ft., passive Perception 11
Languages any languages it knew in life
Challenge 4 (1,100 XP)

Ethereal Sight. The ghost can see 60 ft. into the Ethereal Plane when it is on the Material Plane, and vice versa.

Incorporeal Movement. The ghost can move through other creatures and objects as if they were difficult terrain. It takes 5 (1d10) force damage if it ends its turn inside an object.

ACTIONS

Withering Touch. *Melee Weapon Attack:* +5 to hit, reach 5 ft., one target. *Hit:* 17 (4d6 + 3) necrotic damage.

Etherealness. The ghost enters the Ethereal Plane from the Material Plane, or vice versa. It is visible on the Material Plane while it is in the Border Ethereal, and vice versa, yet it can't affect or be affected by anything on the other plane.

Horrifying Visage. Each non-undead creature within 60 ft. of the ghost that can see it must succeed on a DC 13 Wisdom saving throw or be frightened for 1 minute. If the save fails by 5 or more, the target also ages 1d4 x 10 years. A frightened target can repeat the saving throw at the end of each of its turns, ending the frightened condition on itself on a success. If a target's saving throw is successful or the effect ends for it, the target is immune to this ghost's Horrifying Visage for the next 24 hours. The aging effect can be reversed with a greater restoration spell, but only within 24 hours of it occurring.

Possession (Recharge 6). One humanoid that the ghost can see within 5 ft. of it must succeed on a DC 13 Charisma saving throw or be possessed by the ghost; the ghost then disappears, and the target is incapacitated and loses control of its body. The ghost now controls the body but doesn't deprive the target of awareness. The ghost can't be targeted by any attack, spell, or other effect, except ones that turn undead, and it retains its alignment, Intelligence, Wisdom, Charisma, and immunity to being charmed and frightened. It otherwise uses the possessed target's statistics, but doesn't gain access to the target's knowledge, class features, or proficiencies.

The possession lasts until the body drops to 0 hit points, the ghost ends it as a bonus action, or the ghost is turned or forced out by an effect like the dispel evil and good spell. When the possession ends, the ghost reappears in an unoccupied space within 5 ft. of the body. The target is immune to this ghost's Possession for 24 hours after succeeding on the saving throw or after the possession ends.

Ghost, Headless

Rumor has it that there are actually two **Headless Ghosts** who were brothers, in life. In a fight over a small treasure chest that they found in the woods near their home, they attacked each other. Although there were no witnesses to the fight, the two brothers were found headless in the woods, both gripping the chest of gold. Local legend is that—in their greed—they both somehow managed to strike the other in the neck with their short swords, ending their lives simultaneously. Because the chest of gold was empty when it was discovered, it is more likely that some wayfaring thief encountered the two brothers, killed them and stole their treasure. Regardless, the two brothers died grisly deaths and still haunt the woods and ruined village and houses where they once lived.

GHOST, HEADLESS
Medium undead, any alignment

Armor Class 11
Hit Points 45 (10d8)
Speed 0 ft., fly 40 ft. (hover)

STR	DEX	CON	INT	WIS	CHA
7 (-2)	13 (+1)	10 (+0)	10 (+0)	12 (+1)	17 (+3)

Damage Resistances acid, fire, lightning, thunder; bludgeoning, piercing, and slashing from nonmagical weapons
Damage Immunities cold, necrotic, poison
Condition Immunities charmed, exhaustion, frightened, grappled, paralyzed, petrified, poisoned, prone, restrained
Senses darkvision 60 ft., passive Perception 11
Languages any languages it knew in life
Challenge 4 (1,100 XP)

Ethereal Sight. The ghost can see 60 ft. into the Ethereal Plane when it is on the Material Plane, and vice versa.

Incorporeal Movement. The ghost can move through other creatures and objects as if they were difficult terrain. It takes 5 (1d10) force damage if it ends its turn inside an object.

ACTIONS

Withering Touch. *Melee Weapon Attack:* +5 to hit, reach 5 ft., one target. *Hit:* 17 (4d6 + 3) necrotic damage.

Ethereainess. The ghost enters the Ethereal Plane from the Material Plane, or vice versa. It is visible on the Material Plane while it is in the Border Ethereal, and vice versa, yet it can't affect or be affected by anything on the other plane.

Horrifying Visage. Each non-undead creature within 60 ft. of the ghost that can see it must succeed on a DC 13 Wisdom saving throw or be frightened for 1 minute. If the save fails by 5 or more, the target also ages 1d4 x 10 years. A frightened target can repeat the saving throw at the end of each of its turns, ending the frightened condition on itself on a success. If a target's saving throw is successful or the effect ends for it, the target is immune to this ghost's Horrifying Visage for the next 24 hours. The aging effect can be reversed with a greater restoration spell, but only within 24 hours of it occurring.

Possession (Recharge 6). One humanoid that the ghost can see within 5 ft. of it must succeed on a DC 13 Charisma saving throw or be possessed by the ghost; the ghost then disappears, and the target is incapacitated and loses control of its body. The ghost now controls the body but doesn't deprive the target of awareness. The ghost can't be targeted by any attack, spell, or other effect, except ones that turn undead, and it retains its alignment, Intelligence, Wisdom, Charisma, and immunity to being charmed and frightened. It otherwise uses the possessed target's statistics, but doesn't gain access to the target's knowledge, class features, or proficiencies.

The possession lasts until the body drops to 0 hit points, the ghost ends it as a bonus action, or the ghost is turned or forced out by an effect like the dispel evil and good spell. When the possession ends, the ghost reappears in an unoccupied space within 5 ft. of the body. The target is immune to this ghost's Possession for 24 hours after succeeding on the saving throw or after the possession ends.

Ghost, Ridgeway

The **Ridgeway Ghost** is a particularly evil, sadistic ghost. Wielding a whip, the ghost will attempt to lure a party member away from the rest of the party and to whip and torture it mercilessly until it eventually dies.

GHOST, RIDGEWAY
Medium undead, any alignment

Armor Class 11
Hit Points 45 (10d8)
Speed 0 ft., fly 40 ft. (hover)

STR	DEX	CON	INT	WIS	CHA
7 (-2)	13 (+1)	10 (+0)	10 (+0)	12 (+1)	17 (+3)

Damage Resistances acid, fire, lightning, thunder; bludgeoning, piercing, and slashing from nonmagical weapons
Damage Immunities cold, necrotic, poison
Condition Immunities charmed, exhaustion, frightened, grappled, paralyzed, petrified, poisoned, prone, restrained
Senses darkvision 60 ft., passive Perception 11
Languages any languages it knew in life
Challenge 4 (1,100 XP)

Ethereal Sight. The ghost can see 60 ft. into the Ethereal Plane when it is on the Material Plane, and vice versa.

Incorporeal Movement. The ghost can move through other creatures and objects as if they were difficult terrain. It takes 5 (1d10) force damage if it ends its turn inside an object.

ACTIONS

Withering Touch. *Melee Weapon Attack:* +5 to hit, reach 5 ft., one target. *Hit:* 17 (4d6 + 3) necrotic damage.

Etherealness. The ghost enters the Ethereal Plane from the Material Plane, or vice versa. It is visible on the Material Plane while it is in the Border Ethereal, and vice versa, yet it can't affect or be affected by anything on the other plane.

Horrifying Visage. Each non-undead creature within 60 ft. of the ghost that can see it must succeed on a DC 13 Wisdom saving throw or be frightened for 1 minute. If the save fails by 5 or more, the target also ages 1d4 x 10 years. A frightened target can repeat the saving throw at the end of each of its turns, ending the frightened condition on itself on a success. If a target's saving throw is successful or the effect ends for it, the target is immune to this ghost's Horrifying Visage for the next 24 hours. The aging effect can be reversed with a greater restoration spell, but only within 24 hours of it occurring.

Possession (Recharge 6). One humanoid that the ghost can see within 5 ft. of it must succeed on a DC 13 Charisma saving throw or be possessed by the ghost; the ghost then disappears, and the target is incapacitated and loses control of its body. The ghost now controls the body but doesn't deprive the target of awareness. The ghost can't be targeted by any attack, spell, or other effect, except ones that turn undead, and it retains its alignment, Intelligence, Wisdom, Charisma, and immunity to being charmed and frightened. It otherwise uses the possessed target's statistics, but doesn't gain access to the target's knowledge, class features, or proficiencies.
   The possession lasts until the body drops to 0 hit points, the ghost ends it as a bonus action, or the ghost is turned or forced out by an effect like the dispel evil and good spell. When the possession ends, the ghost reappears in an unoccupied space within 5 ft. of the body. The target is immune to this ghost's Possession for 24 hours after succeeding on the saving throw or after the possession ends.

Gruagach

Gruagach is seldom seen other than in the northern-most reaches of *Legendaria*. Although some report encounters with Gruagach, none have actually seen it. The Gruagach is rumored to join parties in humanoid form, choosing an opportune time to shape-change into a wolf or wolf-humanoid and rip its prey to shreds—before disappearing into the night.

GRUAGACH
Medium humanoid, Chaotic Evil

Armor Class 11 (natural armor)
Hit Points 58 (9d8+18)
Speed 30 ft. (40' in wolf form)

STR	DEX	CON	INT	WIS	CHA
15 (+2)	13 (+1)	14 (+2)	10 (+0)	11 (+0)	10 (+0)

Skills Perception +2, Stealth +3
Damage Immunities bludgeoning, piercing, and slashing from nonmagical attacks that aren't silvered
Condition Immunities poisoned
Senses darkvision 60 ft., passive Perception 12
Languages Common
Challenge 3 (700 XP)

Shapechanger. Can morph into a wolf-humanoid hybrid, or a wolf. Statistics are the same for each form.

Keen Hearing and Smell. Advantage on all Wisdom (Perception) checks that rely on hearing or smell.

ACTIONS

Multiattack. Makes 2 attacks: one bite and one with claw or spear.

Bite (wolf or hybrid only). +4, 5' reach; Hit: 6 (1d8+2) piercing. Humanoids save on DC 12 Constitution or be cursed with lycanthropy.

Claws (Hybrid or Wolf form only). +4 to hit, reach 5'. Hit: 7 (2d4+2) slashing damage.

Spear (Humanoid Only). +4 to hit, 5' reach or 20/60' range; Hit: 7 (2d4+2) piercing damage, or 6 (1d8+2) piercing damage if used with two hands to make a melee attack.

Grýla

Grýla is a particularly dangerous night hag. She is adept at scribing magical scrolls and has the power to charm party members into acting on thoughts and emotions they might otherwise ignore. The slightest of emotions can be magnified many times over by Grýla.

GRYLA
Medium fiend, neutral evil

Armor Class 17 (natural armor)
Hit Points 112 (15d8 + 45)
Speed 30 ft.

STR	DEX	CON	INT	WIS	CHA
18 (+4)	15 (+2)	16 (+3)	16 (+3)	14 (+2)	16 (+3)

Skills Deception +6, Insight +5, Perception +5, Stealth +5
Damage Resistances cold, fire; bludgeoning, piercing, and slashing from nonmagical weapons that aren't silvered
Condition Immunities charmed
Senses darkvision 120 ft., passive Perception 15
Languages Abyssal, Common, Infernal, Primordial
Challenge 5 (1,800 XP)

Innate Spellcasting. The hag's innate spellcasting ability is Charisma (spell save DC 14, +6 to hit with spell attacks). She can innately cast the following spells, requiring no material components:

At will: *detect magic, magic missile*
2/day each: *plane shift* (self only), *ray of enfeeblement, sleep*

Magic Resistance. The hag has advantage on saving throws against spells and other magical effects.

Night Hag Items. A night hag carries two very rare magic items that she must craft for herself If either object is lost, the night hag will go to great lengths to retrieve it, as creating a new tool takes time and effort.
   Heartstone: This lustrous black gem allows a night hag to become ethereal while it is in her possession. The touch of a heartstone also cures any disease. Crafting a heartstone takes 30 days.
   Soul Bag: When an evil humanoid dies as a result of a night hag's Nightmare Haunting, the hag catches the soul in this black sack made of stitched flesh. A soul bag can hold only one evil soul at a time, and only the night hag who crafted the bag can catch a soul with it. Crafting a soul bag takes 7 days and a humanoid sacrifice (whose flesh is used to make the bag).

Hag Coven. When hags must work together, they form covens, in spite of their selfish natures. A coven is made up of hags of any type, all of whom are equals within the group. However, each of the hags continues to desire more personal power.
   A coven consists of three hags so that any arguments between two hags can be settled by the third. If more than three hags ever come together, as might happen if two covens come into conflict, the result is usually chaos.

Shared Spellcasting (Coven Only). While all three members of a hag coven are within 30 feet of one another, they can each cast the following spells from the wizard's spell list but must share the spell slots among themselves:

1st level (4 slots): *identify, ray of sickness*
2nd level (3 slots): *hold person, locate object*
3rd level (3 slots): *bestow curse, counterspell, lightning bolt*
4th level (3 slots): *phantasmal killer, polymorph*
5th level (2 slots): *contact other plane, scrying*
6th level (1 slot): *eye bite*

   For casting these spells, each hag is a 12th-level spellcaster that uses Intelligence as her spellcasting ability. The spell save DC is 12+the hag's Intelligence modifier, and the spell attack bonus is 4+the hag's Intelligence modifier.

Hag Eye (Coven Only). A hag coven can craft a magic item called a hag eye, which is made from a real eye coated in varnish and often fitted to a pendant or other wearable item. The hag eye is usually entrusted to a minion for safekeeping and transport. A hag in the coven can take an action to see what the hag eye sees if the hag eye is on the same plane of existence. A hag eye has AC 10, 1 hit point, and darkvision with a radius of 60 feet. If it is destroyed, each coven member takes 3d10 psychic damage and is blinded for 24 hours.
   A hag coven can have only one hag eye at a time, and creating a new one requires all three members of the coven to perform a ritual. The ritual takes 1 hour, and the hags can't perform it while blinded. During the ritual, if the hags take any action other than performing the ritual, they must start over.

ACTIONS

Claws (Hag Form Only). Melee Weapon Attack: +7 to hit, reach 5 ft., one target. Hit: 13 (2d8 + 4) slashing damage.

Change Shape. The hag magically polymorphs into a Small or Medium female humanoid, or back into her true form. Her statistics are the same in each form. Any equipment she is wearing or carrying isn't transformed. She reverts to her true form if she dies.

Ethfrom. The hag magically enters the Ethereal Plane from the Material Plane, or vice versa. To do so, the hag must have a heartstone in her possession.

Nightmare Haunting (1/Day). While on the Ethereal Plane, the hag magically touches a sleeping humanoid on the Material Plane. A protection from evil and good spell cast on the target prevents this contact, as does a magic circle. As long as the contact persists, the target has dreadful visions. If these visions last for at least 1 hour, the target gains no benefit from its rest, and its hit point maximum is reduced by 5 (1d10). If this effect reduces the target's hit point maximum to 0, the target dies, and if the target was evil, its soul is trapped in the hag's soul bag. The reduction to the target's hit point maximum lasts until removed by the greater restoration spell or similar magic.

Hans Trapp

Hans Trapp has a reputation as a master butcher. Tall, muscular and middle-aged, his appearance will match his profession. His butcher's apron will be covered in blood and gore. However, that reputation hides a deeper secret: that Hans Trapp is dangerous in his callous killing. He will attempt to endear himself to the party by sharing secrets with them so that he might later single out those party members most threaten him—so that he may kill them. Hans Trapp is very concerned about self-preservation and will flee if he feels out-powered in any way. Rumor has it that Hans Trapp has amassed a great fortune.

HANS TRAPP
Medium elemental, neutral

Armor Class 14
Hit Points 104 (16d8 + 32)
Speed 50 ft., fly 50 ft. (hover)

STR	DEX	CON	INT	WIS	CHA
16 (+3)	19 (+4)	14 (+2)	10 (+0)	15 (+2)	11 (+0)

Skills Perception +8, Stealth +10
Damage Resistances bludgeoning, piercing, and slashing from nonmagical weapons
Damage Immunities poison
Condition Immunities exhaustion, grappled, paralyzed, petrified, poisoned, prone, restrained, unconscious
Senses darkvision 60 ft., passive Perception 18
Languages Common
Challenge 6 (2,300 XP)

Invisibility. hans trapp is invisible.

Faultless Tracker. hans trapp is given a quarry by its summoner. hans trapp knows the direction and distance to its quarry as long as the two of them are on the same plane of existence. hans trapp also knows the location of its summoner.

ACTIONS

Multiattack. hans trapp makes two slam attacks.

Slam. *Melee Weapon Attack:* +6 to hit, reach 5 ft., one target. *Hit:* 10 (2d6 + 3) bludgeoning damage.

Haunchies of Muskego

The **Haunchies** appear as overgrown human children and will initially attempt to deceive parties into thinking that they are in distress and in need of aid. Their attacks are swift and deadly, though at heart they are quite cowardly and will quickly retreat if they feel an encounter is not going to end to their advantage.

HAUNCHIES OF MUSKEGO
Small humanoid (goblinoid), neutral evil

Armor Class 17 (chain shirt, shield)
Hit Points 21 (6d6)
Speed 30 ft.

STR	DEX	CON	INT	WIS	CHA
10 (+0)	14 (+2)	10 (+0)	10 (+0)	8 (-1)	10 (+0)

Skills Stealth +6
Senses darkvision 60 ft., passive Perception 9
Languages Common, Goblin
Challenge 1 (200 XP)

Nimble Escape. The haunchies of muskego can take the Disengage or Hide action as a bonus action on each of its turns.

ACTIONS

Scimitar. *Melee Weapon Attack:* +4 to hit, reach 5 ft., one target. *Hit:* 5 (1d6 + 2) slashing damage.

Shortbow. *Ranged Weapon Attack:* +4 to hit, range 80/320 ft., one target. *Hit:* 5 (1d6 + 2) piercing damage.

REACTIONS

Redirect Attack. When a creature the haunchies of muskego can see targets it with an attack, the haunchies of muskego chooses another haunchies of muskego within 5' of it. The two swap places, and the chosen haunchies of muskego becomes the target instead.

Hodag

No living soul has ever actually seen a **Hodag**, though there are some who claim they have. It resembles something of a cross between a large, horned lizard and a dragon. The Hodag will use its legendary speed, especially when flying, to its advantage.

HODAG

Large monstrosity (hodag), Evil

Armor Class 16 (natural armor)
Hit Points 136 (16d10+48)
Speed 30 ft., fly 80 ft., swim 40 ft.

STR	DEX	CON	INT	WIS	CHA
19 (+4)	12 (+1)	17 (+3)	16 (+3)	13 (+1)	15 (+2)

Skills Perception +5, Stealth +5
Damage Immunities lightning
Senses darkvision 90 ft., passive Perception 15
Languages Draconic
Challenge 11 (7,200 XP)

ACTIONS

Multiattack. 2 attacks: one bite, and one to constrict.

Bite. +10 to hit, 5' reach; Hit: 22 (3d10+6) piercing.

Constrict. +10 to hit, 5' reach;17 (2d10+6) bludgeoning plus 17 (2d10+6) slashing. Target is grappled. DC 16 to escape.

Lightening Breath (Recharge 5-6). Exhales a line of lightening 20' long and 5' wide. DC 16 Dexterity save, taking 66 HP (12d10) lightening damage, or half as much on success.

Swallow. If grappled, bite attack results in target being swallowed. Target is blind and restrained and takes 21 (6d6) acid damage at the beginning of every turn. If Thrakos takes 30 HP damage or more on a single turn, it must succeed on a DC 14 Constitution save or regurgitate the target.

Jòlakötturinn

The **Jòlakötturinn** tend to live and hunt around cavernous lairs, the ground of which tends to be strewn with the bones of its prey. It will often seek to attack with some element of surprise and will quickly retreat if it feels outnumbered.

JOLAKOTTURINN

Large fiend, chaotic evil

Armor Class 14 (natural armor)
Hit Points 110 (14d10 + 40)
Speed 50 ft., climb 30 ft.

STR	DEX	CON	INT	WIS	CHA
17 (+3)	16 (+3)	16 (+3)	15 (+2)	16 (+3)	15 (+2)

Skills Perception +6, Stealth +6
Damage Resistances cold, fire, lightning; bludgeoning, piercing, and slashing from nonmagical attacks
Condition Immunities charmed, frightened, poisoned
Senses darkvision 60 ft., tremorsense 120 ft., passive Perception 16
Languages Abyssal, Common, Gnoll, telepathy 120 ft.
Challenge 8 (3,900 XP)

ACTIONS

Multiattack. The jolakotturinn makes two claw attacks and two stinger attacks.

Claw. *Melee Weapon Attack:* +8 to hit, reach 5 ft., one target. *Hit:* 12 (2d6 + 5) slashing damage.

Stinger. *Melee Weapon Attack:* +8 to hit, reach 5 ft., one creature. *Hit:* 12 (2d6 + 5) piercing damage, and the target must succeed on a DC 15 Charisma saving throw or have its fate corrupted. A creature with corrupted fate has disadvantage on Charisma checks and Charisma saving throws, and it is immune to divination spells and to effects that sense emotions or read thoughts. The target's fate can be restored by a dispel evil and good spell or comparable magic.

Invisibility. The jolakotturinn turns invisible until it attacks or casts a spell, or until its concentration ends. Equipment the jolakotturinn wears or carries becomes invisible with it.

Krake

In some limited and very isolated areas of *Legendaria* there are reports of a class of crows that are exceptionally intelligent, large for their size and aggressive. As legends have it, the **krake** will attack other birds and fight until they have not only killed them, but completely destroyed them. Krake are cowardly in isolation, but absolutely fearless in large flocks which can easily number in the hundreds. When sighted, it has been said that their numbers will darken the daytime sky. If **Chogan** summons them, consider no less than **1D100+50** of them in a flock, if not higher.

KRAKE
Medium beast, unaligned

Armor Class 11 (natural armor)
Hit Points 7 (1d8 + 3)
Speed 10 ft., fly 60 ft.

STR	DEX	CON	INT	WIS	CHA
7 (-2)	10 (+0)	14 (+2)	2 (-4)	12 (+1)	4 (-3)

Skills Perception +3
Senses blindsight 10 ft., darkvision 25 ft., passive Perception 13
Languages —
Challenge 1 (200 XP)

Keen Sight and Smell. The krake has advantage on Wisdom (Perception) checks that rely on sight or smell.

Pack Tactics. The krake has advantage on an attack roll against a creature if at least one of the krake's allies is within 5 ft. of the creature and the ally isn't incapacitated.

ACTIONS

Beak. *Melee Weapon Attack:* +2 to hit, reach 5 ft., one target. *Hit:* 2 (1d4) piercing damage.

Krampus

A dangerous enough demon in its own right, **Krampus** will use illusion to deceive the party before attacking. If there are other demons in the area, Krampus will summon them to his aid.

KRAMPUS
Huge fiend (demon), chaotic evil

Armor Class 19 (natural armor)
Hit Points 262 (21d12 + 126)
Speed 40 ft., fly 80 ft.

STR	DEX	CON	INT	WIS	CHA
26 (+8)	15 (+2)	22 (+6)	20 (+5)	16 (+3)	22 (+6)

Saving Throws Str +14, Con +12, Wis +9, Cha +12
Damage Resistances cold, lightning; bludgeoning, piercing, and slashing from nonmagical weapons
Damage Immunities fire, poison
Condition Immunities poisoned
Senses truesight 120 ft., passive Perception 13
Languages Abyssal, telepathy 120 ft.
Challenge 19 (22,000 XP)

Death Throes. When the krampus dies, it explodes, and each creature within 30 feet of it must make a DC 20 Dexterity saving throw, taking 70 (20d6) fire damage on a failed save, or half as much damage on a successful one. The explosion ignites flammable objects in that area that aren't being worn or carried, and it destroys the krampus's weapons.

Fire Aura. At the start of each of the krampus's turns, each creature within 5 feet of it takes 10 (3d6) fire damage, and flammable objects in the aura that aren't being worn or carried ignite. A creature that touches the krampus or hits it with a melee attack while within 5 feet of it takes 10 (3d6) fire damage.

Magic Resistance. The krampus has advantage on saving throws against spells and other magical effects.

Magic Weapons. The krampus's weapon attacks are magical.

ACTIONS

Multiattack. Thekrampus makes two attacks: one with its longsword and one with its whip.

Longsword. *Melee Weapon Attack:* +14 to hit, reach 10 ft., one target. *Hit:* 21 (3d8 + 8) slashing damage plus 13 (3d8) lightning damage. If the balor scores a critical hit, it rolls damage dice three times, instead of twice.

Whip. *Melee Weapon Attack:* +14 to hit, reach 30 ft., one target. *Hit:* 15 (2d6 + 8) slashing damage plus 10 (3d6) fire damage, and the target must succeed on a DC 20 Strength saving throw or be pulled up to 25 feet toward the balor.

Teleport. The krampus magically teleports, along with any equipment it is wearing or carrying, up to 120 feet to an unoccupied space it can see.

Lake Monster, Pepie

Pepie the Lake Monster has been reported under only the most questionable of circumstances: typically, during storms. Those reporting having seen Pepie will report large, grey crests of the creature's back, and nothing more. The reports are typically dismissed because of such poor visibility and are most often attributed to mistaking choppy water for the beast's form.

PEPIE THE LAKE MONSTER
Large monstrosity, evil

Armor Class 18 (natural armor)
Hit Points 195 (17d12 + 85)
Speed 30 ft., swim 40 ft.

STR	DEX	CON	INT	WIS	CHA
22 (+6)	13 (+1)	19 (+4)	16 (+3)	16 (+3)	12 (+1)

Saving Throws Con +9, Wis +8, Cha +6
Skills Perception +13
Damage Immunities cold, fire
Condition Immunities paralyzed, unconscious
Senses blindsight 60 ft., darkvision 90 ft., passive Perception 23
Languages Common, Draconic
Challenge 14 (11,500 XP)

Amphibious. The pepie the lake monster can breathe air and water.

Legendary Resistance (3/Day). If the pepie the lake monster fails a saving throw, it can choose to succeed instead.

ACTIONS

Multiattack. The pepie the lake monster can use its Frightful Presence. It then makes three attacks: one with its bite and two with its fins and tail.

Bite. *Melee Weapon Attack:* +11 to hit, reach 10 ft., one target. *Hit:* 17 (2d10 + 6) piercing damage plus 4 (1d8) acid damage.

Tail and Fins. *Melee Weapon Attack:* +11 to hit, reach 15 ft., one target. *Hit:* 15 (2d8 + 6) bludgeoning damage.

Frightful Presence. Each creature of the pepie the lake monster's choice that is within 120 feet of the dragon and aware of it must succeed on a DC 16 Wisdom saving throw or become frightened for 1 minute. A creature can repeat the saving throw at the end of each of its turns, ending the effect on itself on a success. If a creature's saving throw is successful or the effect ends for it, the creature is immune to the pepie the lake monster's Frightful Presence for the next 24 hours.

REACTIONS

Regeneration. Regains 15 HP at the start of every round, unless its head has been severed.

Lake Leap. When submerged in water, can transfer to a body of water as a bonus action up to 1,000' away.

Lake Winnebago Monster

Many of the sea and freshwater creatures of *Legendaria* are the stuff of myth and legend because few survive their brutal attacks. The **Lake Winnebago Monster** is no different: it will typically be drawn from its depths during storms when party members are disoriented and already fighting for survival. The monster has no desire to kill for the sake of killing as much as to feed. Its attacks will focus on disorientation and getting party members into the water so that it may devour them whole.

LAKE WINNEBAGO MONSTER
Huge monstrosity, evil

Armor Class 18 (natural armor)
Hit Points 472 (27d20 + 189)
Speed 20 ft., swim 60 ft.

STR	DEX	CON	INT	WIS	CHA
30 (+10)	11 (+0)	25 (+7)	22 (+6)	18 (+4)	20 (+5)

Saving Throws Str +17, Dex +7, Con +14, Int +13, Wis +11
Damage Immunities lightning; bludgeoning, piercing, and slashing from nonmagical weapons
Condition Immunities frightened, paralyzed
Senses truesight 120 ft., passive Perception 14
Languages and Primordial but can't speak, Infernal, telepathy 120 ft.
Challenge 23 (50,000 XP)

Amphibious. The lake winnebago monster can breathe air and water.

Freedom of Movement. The lake winnebago monster ignores difficult terrain, and magical effects can't reduce its speed or cause it to be restrained. It can spend 5 feet of movement to escape from nonmagical restraints or being grappled.

Siege Monster. The lake winnebago monster deals double damage to objects and structures.

ACTIONS

Multiattack. The lake winnebago monster makes one tail attacks, which it can replace with one use of Fling, and two bites.

Bite. *Melee Weapon Attack:* +7 to hit, reach 5 ft., one target. *Hit:* 23 (3d8 + 10) piercing damage. If the target is a Large or smaller creature grappled by the lake winnebago monster, that creature is swallowed, and the grapple ends. While swallowed, the creature is blinded and restrained, it has total cover against attacks and other effects outside the lake winnebago monster, and it takes 42 (12d6) acid damage at the start of each of the lake winnebago monster's turns. If the lake winnebago monster takes 50 damage or more on a single turn from a creature inside it, the lake winnebago monster must succeed on a DC 25 Constitution saving throw at the end of that turn or regurgitate all swallowed creatures, which fall prone in a space within 10 feet of the lake winnebago monster. If the lake winnebago monster dies, a swallowed creature is no longer restrained by it and can escape from the corpse using 15 feet of movement, exiting prone.

Fling. One Large or smaller object held or creature grappled by the kraken is thrown up to 60 feet in a random direction and knocked prone. If a thrown target strikes a solid surface, the target takes 3 (1d6) bludgeoning damage for every 10 feet it was thrown. If the target is thrown at another creature, that creature must succeed on a DC 18 Dexterity saving throw or take the same damage and be knocked prone.

Lich (Keraptis)

Keraptis is an evil wizard that once ruled all of the land surrounding *White Plume Mountain* for hundreds of years. After having disappeared for nearly as long, there are again rumors that Keraptis is once again trying to assert his control over his old kingdom. Rumor has it his lair is deep within White Plume Mountain, where he is amassing an army of demons and undead to help him rule over his dominion.

LICH (KERAPTIS)
Medium undead, any evil alignment

Armor Class 17 (natural armor)
Hit Points 135 (18d8 + 54)
Speed 30 ft.

STR	DEX	CON	INT	WIS	CHA
11 (+0)	16 (+3)	16 (+3)	20 (+5)	14 (+2)	16 (+3)

Saving Throws Con +10, Int +12, Wis +9
Skills Arcana +19, History +12, Insight +9, Perception +9
Damage Resistances cold, lightning, necrotic
Damage Immunities poison; bludgeoning, piercing, and slashing from nonmagical weapons
Condition Immunities charmed, exhaustion, frightened, paralyzed, poisoned
Senses truesight 120 ft., passive Perception 19
Languages Common plus up to five other languages
Challenge 21 (33,000 XP)

Legendary Resistance (3/Day). If the lich fails a saving throw, it can choose to succeed instead.

Rejuvenation. If it has a phylactery, a destroyed lich gains a new body in 1d10 days, regaining all its hit points and becoming active again. The new body appears within 5 feet of the phylactery.

Spellcasting. The lich is an 18th-level spellcaster. Its spellcasting ability is Intelligence (spell save DC 20, +12 to hit with spell attacks). The lich has the following wizard spells prepared:

Cantrips (at will): *mage hand, prestidigitation, ray of frost*
1st level (4 slots): *detect magic, magic missile, shield, thunderwave*
2nd level (3 slots): *detect thoughts, invisibility, Melf's acid arrow, mirror image*
3rd level (3 slots): *animate dead, counterspell, dispel magic, fireball*
4th level (3 slots): *blight, dimension door*
5th level (3 slots): *cloudkill, scrying*
6th level (1 slot): *disintegrate, globe of invulnerability*
7th level (1 slot): *finger of death, plane shift*
8th level (1 slot): *dominate monster, power word stun*
9th level (1 slot): *power word kill*

Turn Resistance. The lich has advantage on saving throws against any effect that turns undead.

ACTIONS

Paralyzing Touch. *Melee Spell Attack:* +12 to hit, reach 5 ft., one creature. *Hit:* 10 (3d6) cold damage. The target must succeed on a DC 18 Constitution saving throw or be paralyzed for 1 minute. The target can repeat the saving throw at the end of each of its turns, ending the effect on itself on a success.

LEGENDARY ACTIONS

The lich can take 3 legendary actions, choosing from the options below. Only one legendary action option can be used at a time and only at the end of another creature's turn. The lich regains spent legendary actions at the start of its turn.

Cantrip. The lich casts a cantrip.
Paralyzing Touch (Costs 2 Actions). The lich uses its Paralyzing Touch.
Frightening Gaze (Costs 2 Actions). The lich fixes its gaze on one creature it can see within 10 feet of it. The target must succeed on a DC 18 Wisdom saving throw against this magic or become frightened for 1 minute. The frightened target can repeat the saving throw at the end of each of its turns, ending the effect on itself on a success. If a target's saving throw is successful or the effect ends for it, the target is immune to the lich's gaze for the next 24 hours.
Disrupt Life (Costs 3 Actions). Each living creature within 20 feet of the lich must make a DC 18 Constitution saving throw against this magic, taking 21 (6d6) necrotic damage on a failed save, or half as much damage on a successful one.

Makwa (Bear)

A fearsome warrior, **Makwa** will attempt to over-power those he attacks. His sheer physical presence is absolutely terrifying. Makwa will plan his attacks carefully and is frightfully swift and merciless.

A FRIEND TO MISAKOKOJISH. **Makwa** is allied with **Misakokojish** and will come to his aid (teleportation) within two turns.

MAKWA
Huge fey (deity), Chaotic

Armor Class 22 (natural armor)
Hit Points 253 (22d12+110)
Speed 60 ft., climb 15 ft., swim 15 ft.

STR	DEX	CON	INT	WIS	CHA
24 (+7)	16 (+3)	20 (+5)	10 (+0)	18 (+4)	18 (+4)

Saving Throws Str +14, Dex +10, Con +12
Skills Athletics +14, Intimidation +18, Nature +14, Perception +18, Stealth +10, Survival +11
Damage Resistances bludgeoning, force
Damage Immunities bludgeoning, piercing, and slashing from nonmagical attacks
Condition Immunities charmed, frightened, prone, restrained, stunned, unconscious
Senses blindsight 30 ft., darkvision 80 ft., truesight 60 ft., passive Perception 28
Languages Celestial, Common, Primordial, telepathy 30 ft.
Challenge 21 (33,000 XP)

Legendary Resistance (3/Day). If the makwa fails a saving throw, it can choose to succeed instead.

Multiattack. The makwa can use its Frightful Presence. It then makes three attacks: one with its bite and two with its claws.

Charge. If the makwa moves at least 20' toward a target and hits it with either a bit or a claw, the target must succeed on a DC 18 Strength save or be knocked prone.

Magic Resistance. makwa has advantage on saving throws against spells and other magical effects.

ACTIONS

Bite. *Melee Weapon Attack:*+ 15 to hit, reach 15 ft., one target. *Hit:* 19 (2d10 + 8) piercing damage plus 9 (2d8) acid damage.

Claw. *Melee Weapon Attack:* +15 to hit, reach 10 ft., one target. *Hit:* 15 (2d6 + 8) slashing damage.

Tail. *Melee Weapon Attack:* +15 to hit, reach 10 ft ., one target. *Hit:* 17 (2d8 + 8) bludgeoning damage.

Frightful Presence. Each creature of the makwa's choice that is within 120 feet of the makwa and aware of it must succeed on a DC 19 Wisdom saving throw or become frightened for 1 minute. A creature can repeat the saving throw at the end of each of its turns, ending the effect on itself on a success. If a creature's saving throw is successful or the effect ends for it, the creature is immune to the dragon's Frightful Presence for the next 24 hours.

Acid Breath (Recharge 5-6). The makwa exhales acid in a 90-foot line that is 10 feet wide. Each creature in that line must make a DC 22 Dexterity saving throw, taking 67 (15d8) acid damage on a failed save, or half as much damage on a successful one.

REACTIONS

Deflect Missiles (Humanoid Form Only). When makwa is hit by a ranged weapon, he can reduce the damage by 25 (1d10+20). If the damage is reduced to 0, he can choose to catch the missile, and then throw it as a ranged attack as part of the same reaction. The missile is +10 to hit and deals 18 (3d8+5) damage.

LEGENDARY ACTIONS

The [MON] can take 3 legendary actions, choosing from the options below. Only one legendary action option can be used at a time and only at the end of another creature's turn. The [MON] regains spent legendary actions at the start of its turn.

Detect. The makwa makes a Wisdom (Perception) check.
Tail Attack. The makwa makes a tail attack.
Rears Up and Entrenches (Costs 2 Actions). The makwa rears up on its hind legs and entrenches. Each creature within 10 ft. of the makwa must succeed on a DC 23 Dexterity saving throw or take 15 (2d6 + 8) bludgeoning damage and be knocked prone. The makwa can then move up to half its speed.

Mashenomak

Mashenomak are commonly found where there are other fish. They are opportunistic and will seldom attack first, relying on larger foe to make the attacks that will drag prey into the water where they will then swarm and attack. Mashenomak are often found in very large schools, numbering **D20+20** or larger.

MASHENOMAK
Medium beast (Fish Swarm), Unaligned

Armor Class 14 (natural armor)
Hit Points 104 (11d8+55)
Speed 0 ft., swim 60 ft.

STR	DEX	CON	INT	WIS	CHA
22 (+6)	13 (+1)	20 (+5)	2 (-4)	12 (+1)	4 (-3)

Skills Perception +4
Damage Resistances piercing, slashing
Condition Immunities grappled, incapacitated, paralyzed, prone, restrained, stunned
Senses blindsight 10 ft., passive Perception 14
Languages —
Challenge 5 (1,800 XP)

Camoflauge. The mashenomak has advantage on Dexterity (Stealth) checks when underwater.

Pack Tactics. Advantage on attack if an ally is within 5'.

Blade Fins. If mashenomak strikes same target with fins and tail, it does 10 additional necrotic damage and it bleeds for 5 HP per turn for 2 more turns.

Swarm Attack. Attacks on the move: does not provoke attacks of opportunity as long as it attacked on the same turn.

ACTIONS

Multiattack. One fin and one tail attack as long as it moved at least 5' before making first attack.

Fins. +9, 5' reach; Hit: 17 (2d10+6) piercing. Critical hit on a natural 19 or 20.

Tail. +9, 5' reach; Hit: 11 (1d10+6), slashing. Critical hit on a natural 19 or 20.

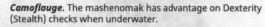

Name: Tim Krause

Minotaur

In their own right, **minotaurs** are a fearsome foe. On *Legendaria*, they are larger, stronger and more intelligent. It is a myth that they only reside in labyrinths and are often found in hilly and forested areas. Their weakness, if any, is that they are unlikely to retreat from battle once they have engaged.

MINOTAUR
Large monstrosity, chaotic evil

Armor Class 14 (natural armor)
Hit Points 76 (9d10 + 27)
Speed 40 ft.

STR	DEX	CON	INT	WIS	CHA
18 (+4)	11 (+0)	16 (+3)	6 (-2)	16 (+3)	9 (-1)

Skills Perception +7
Senses darkvision 60 ft., passive Perception 17
Languages Abyssal
Challenge 3 (700 XP)

Charge. If the minotaur moves at least 10 ft. straight toward a target and then hits it with a gore attack on the same turn, the target takes an extra 9 (2d8) piercing damage. If the target is a creature, it must succeed on a DC 14 Strength saving throw or be pushed up to 10 ft. away and knocked prone.

Labyrinthine Recall. The minotaur can perfectly recall any path it has traveled.

Reckless. At the start of its turn, the minotaur can gain advantage on all melee weapon attack rolls it makes during that turn, but attack rolls against it have advantage until the start of its next turn.

ACTIONS

Greataxe. *Melee Weapon Attack:* +6 to hit, reach 5 ft., one target. *Hit:* 17 (2d12 + 4) slashing damage.

Gore. *Melee Weapon Attack:* +6 to hit, reach 5 ft., one target. *Hit:* 13 (2d8 + 4) piercing damage.

Misakakojish (Badger)

Misakokojish is an isolated deity and will fight alone. He is fiercely independent and often worshiped by rangers, assassins and creatures of the night. If cornered, he will most surely fight to his physical death. He is, however, a master of deception and will attempt to lure his combatants to a lair that will be laden with traps, dead-ends and devices that will teleport the party to deceptively similar locations. The longer a party fights badger the more likely they will go made with confusion.

A FRIEND TO MAKWA. Misakokojish is allied with **Makwa** and will come to his aid (teleportation) within two turns.

MISAKAKOJISH
Huge fey (deity), neutral

Armor Class 20 (natural armor)
Hit Points 187 (15d12+90)
Speed 50 ft., burrow 60 ft., climb 20 ft.

STR	DEX	CON	INT	WIS	CHA
22 (+6)	14 (+2)	22 (+6)	15 (+2)	18 (+4)	19 (+4)

Saving Throws Str +14, Dex +10, Wis +12, Cha +12
Skills Athletics +14, Intimidation +20, Nature +18, Perception +20, Stealth +10, Survival +12
Damage Resistances bludgeoning, force
Damage Immunities bludgeoning, piercing, and slashing from nonmagical attacks
Condition Immunities blinded, frightened, prone, restrained, stunned, unconscious
Senses blindsight 60 ft., darkvision 120 ft., passive Perception 30
Languages Celestial, Common, Primordial, telepathy 30 ft.
Challenge 25 (75,000 XP)

Legendary Resistance (3/Day). If the dragon fails a saving throw, it can choose to succeed instead.

Multiattack. The misakakojish can use its Frightful Presence. It then makes three attacks: one with its bite and two with its claws.

Charge. If the misakakojish moves at least 20' toward a target and hits it with either a bit or a claw, the target must succeed on a DC 18 Strength save or be knocked prone.

Magic Resistance. misakakojish has advantage on saving throws against spells and other magical effects.

ACTIONS

Bite. *Melee Weapon Attack:*+ 15 to hit, reach 15 ft., one target. *Hit:* 19 (2d10 + 8) piercing damage plus 9 (2d8) acid damage.

Claw. *Melee Weapon Attack:* +15 to hit, reach 10 ft., one target. *Hit:* 15 (2d6 + 8) slashing damage.

Tail. *Melee Weapon Attack:* +15 to hit, reach 10 ft., one target. *Hit:* 17 (2d8 + 8) bludgeoning damage.

Frightful Presence. Each creature of the misakakojish's choice that is within 120 feet of the misakakojish and aware of it must succeed on a DC 19 Wisdom saving throw or become frightened for 1 minute. A creature can repeat the saving throw at the end of each of its turns, ending the effect on itself on a success. If a creature's saving throw is successful or the effect ends for it, the creature is immune to the dragon's Frightful Presence for the next 24 hours.

Acid Breath (Recharge 5-6). The misakakojish exhales acid in a 90-foot line that is 10 feet wide. Each creature in that line must make a DC 22 Dexterity saving throw, taking 67 (15d8) acid damage on a failed save, or half as much damage on a successful one.

LEGENDARY ACTIONS

The [MON] can take 3 legendary actions, choosing from the options below. Only one legendary action option can be used at a time and only at the end of another creature's turn. The [MON] regains spent legendary actions at the start of its turn.

Detect. The misakakojish makes a Wisdom (Perception) check.
Tail Attack. The misakakojish makes a tail attack.
Wing Attack (Costs 2 Actions). The dragon beats its wings. Each creature within 15 ft. of the dragon must succeed on a DC 23 Dexterity saving throw or take 15 (2d6 + 8) bludgeoning damage and be knocked prone. The dragon can then fly up to half its flying speed.
Rears Up and Entrenches (Costs 2 Actions). The misakakojish rears up on its hind legs and entrenches. Each creature within 10 ft. of the misakakojish must succeed on a DC 23 Dexterity saving throw or take 15 (2d6 + 8) bludgeoning damage and be knocked prone. The misakakojish can then move up to half its speed.

Morrigan (Elven Archer)

Morrigan is a deadly hunter in that she exists purely to hunt her foe. She has targeted the party and will ruthlessly track them before taking her first shot. She is known by legend only—there are many who would deny her very existence. Whether the party is attacked, or only suspects they are being tracked, they will struggle to find any trace of her passing. Morrigan's only fatal flaw is her almost obsessive desire to collect trophies from all of her hunts. **See the Appendix** for a map of **Morrigan's Lodge of Legendary Hunts.**

MORRIGAN (ELVEN ARCHER)

Medium fey, lawful neutral

Armor Class 17 (studded leather)
Hit Points 97 (18d8 + 14)
Speed 45 ft., climb 10 ft., swim 5 ft.

STR	DEX	CON	INT	WIS	CHA
14 (+2)	21 (+5)	14 (+2)	12 (+1)	14 (+2)	16 (+3)

Saving Throws Dex +9, Con +6
Skills Insight +6, Intimidation +7, Perception +6, Stealth +9, Survival +10
Damage Resistances bludgeoning, piercing, and slashing from nonmagical weapons
Condition Immunities exhaustion, frightened, poisoned
Senses darkvision 60 ft., passive Perception 16
Languages Common, Sylvan
Challenge 9 (5,000 XP)

Forest Sense. While in forest surroundings, morrigan (elven archer) receives a +4 bonus on initiative checks.

Forest Transformation. morrigan (elven archer) can meld into any tree in her forest for as long as she wishes, similar to the meld into stone spell.

Innate Spellcasting. morrigan (elven archer)'s innate spellcasting ability is Charisma (spell save DC 15). She can innately cast the following spells, requiring no material components:

3/day: *sleep*
1/week: *control weather*

ACTIONS

Multiattack. A vila makes two shortsword attacks or two shortbow attacks.

+1 Shortsword. Melee Weapon Attack: +9 to hit, reach 5 ft., one target. *Hit:* 9 (1d6 + 6) piercing damage.

+1 Shortbow. Ranged Weapon Attack: +9 to hit, range 80/320 ft., one target. *Hit:* 9 (1d6 + 6) piercing damage.

Forest Invocation (2/Day). morrigan (elven archer) magically calls 2d6 wolves or 8d6 *Krake*. The called creatures arrive in 1d4 rounds, acting as allies of morrigan (elven archer) and obeying her spoken commands. The beasts remain for 1 hour, until morrigan (elven archer) dies, or until morrigan (elven archer) dismisses them as a bonus action.

Père Fouettard

Père Fouettard wields a whip and is known in particular for his indiscriminate attack on children. He attacks at night and is known to disappear without a trace.

PERE FOUETTARD
Large construct, unaligned

Armor Class 17 (natural armor)
Hit Points 142 (15d10 + 60)
Speed 30 ft.

STR	DEX	CON	INT	WIS	CHA
18 (+4)	8 (-1)	18 (+4)	7 (-2)	10 (+0)	3 (-4)

Damage Immunities poison
Condition Immunities charmed, exhaustion, frightened, paralyzed, poisoned
Senses blindsight 10 ft., darkvision 60 ft., passive Perception 10
Languages understands commands given in any language but can't speak
Challenge 7 (2,900 XP)

Regeneration. The pere fouettard regains 10 hit points at the start of its turn if it has at least 1 hit. point.

Spell Storing. A spellcaster (Krampus) who wears the pere fouettard's amulet can cause the guardian to store one spell of 4th level or lower. To do so, the wearer must cast the spell on the guardian. The spell has no effect but is stored within pere fouettard. When commanded to do so by the wearer or when a situation arises that was predefined by the spellcaster, pere fouettard casts the stored spell with any parameters set by the original caster, requiring no components. When the spell is cast or a new spell is stored, any previously stored spell is lost.

ACTIONS

Multiattack. pere fouettard makes two fist attacks.

Fist. *Melee Weapon Attack:* +7 to hit, reach 5 ft., one target. *Hit:* 11 (2d6 + 4) bludgeoning damage.

REACTIONS

Shield. When a creature makes an attack against Krampus, pere fouettard grants a +2 bonus to the Krampus's AC if pere fouettard is within 5 feet of the wearer.

Quesper – Cleric

Don't let their fearsome looks deceive you: the **Quesper** are rumored to be a very peaceful race, cursed centuries ago by a witch (see **Quespa**). They live in the depths of the swamps of *Legendaria* (see *Appendix*), but will come to the aid of your party, asking for nothing in return. Consider developing a complete side adventure around removing the curse of Quespa. This is primarily a race of fighters, but you could choose to adapt statistics to include members who are healers, herbalists or trackers.

QUESPER - CLERIC

Large dragon, Chaotic Evil

Armor Class 13 (natural armor)
Hit Points 84 (9d10+48)
Speed 40 ft., swim 15 ft.

STR	DEX	CON	INT	WIS	CHA
14 (+2)	12 (+1)	16 (+3)	12 (+1)	16 (+3)	11 (+0)

Saving Throws Con +5, Wis +5
Skills History +3, Perception +5, Religion +3
Damage Resistances slashing; bludgeoning, piercing, and slashing from nonmagical attacks
Condition Immunities poisoned
Senses darkvision 120 ft., passive Perception 15
Languages Common, Draconic
Challenge 4 (1,100 XP)

Camoflauge. The quesper - cleric has advantage on Dexterity (Stealth) checks when underwater.

ACTIONS

Multiattack. The quesper - cleric makes two bite attacks.

Bite. +5 hit, 5' reach; Hit: 10 (2d6+3) piercing damage. Creature is grappled (escape DC 13 strength) until it escapes. The quesper - cleric can only bite grappled target (at advantage).

Hand Axe. +2, 10' reach; Hit: 9 (1d10+4, piercing.

Swamp Incantations. Cantrips (at will): light, poison spray, sacred spray, thaumaturgy
 1st level (4 slots): bless, cure wounds, guiding bolt, shield of faith
 2nd level (3 slots): blindness/deafness, hold person, silence, zone of truth
 3rd level (3 slots): animate dead, feign death, remove curse

Quesper – Mage

QUESPER - MAGE

Large dragon, Chaotic Evil

Armor Class 13 (natural armor)
Hit Points 84 (9d10+48)
Speed 40 ft., swim 15 ft.

STR	DEX	CON	INT	WIS	CHA
14 (+2)	12 (+1)	16 (+3)	16 (+3)	12 (+1)	11 (+0)

Saving Throws Con +5, Int +5
Skills Arcana +5, Perception +3, Survival +3
Damage Resistances slashing; bludgeoning, piercing, and slashing from nonmagical attacks
Condition Immunities poisoned
Senses darkvision 120 ft., passive Perception 13
Languages Common, Draconic
Challenge 4 (1,100 XP)

Camoflauge. The quesper - mage has advantage on Dexterity (Stealth) checks when underwater.

ACTIONS

Multiattack. The quesper - mage makes two bite attacks.

Bite. +5 hit, 5' reach; Hit: 10 (2d6+3) piercing damage. Creature is grappled (escape DC 13 strength) until it escapes. The quesper - mage can only bite grappled target (at advantage).

Hand Axe. +2, 10' reach; Hit: 9 (1d10+4, piercing.

Swamp Spells. Cantrips (at will): acid splash, guidance, swamp flame (sacred flame)
  1st level (4 slots): chromatic orb, disguise self, jump, witch bolt
  2nd level (3 slots): blur, darkness, misty step
  3rd level (3 slots): fear, lightning bot, slow

Quesper – Warrior

Quesper - Warrior

Large dragon, Chaotic Evil

Armor Class 14 (natural armor)
Hit Points 114 (12d10+48)
Speed 40 ft., swim 15 ft.

STR	DEX	CON	INT	WIS	CHA
20 (+5)	12 (+1)	18 (+4)	8 (-1)	10 (+0)	9 (-1)

Saving Throws Str +7, Con +6
Skills Athletics +7
Damage Resistances slashing
Condition Immunities poisoned
Senses darkvision 120 ft., passive Perception 10
Languages Common, Draconic
Challenge 4 (1,100 XP)

Camoflauge. The quesper - warrior has advantage on Dexterity (Stealth) checks when underwater.

Actions

Multiattack. The quesper - warrior makes two bite attacks.

Bite. +5 hit, 5' reach; Hit: 10 (2d6+3) piercing damage. Creature is grappled (escape DC 13 strength) until it escapes. The quesper - warrior can only bite grappled target (at advantage).

Axe. +7, 10' reach; Hit: 16 (2d10+5, piercing. Can choose to push the target away if it fails a DC 16 Strength save.

Rogue

ROGUE

Medium humanoid (any race), chaotic neutral

Armor Class 14 (studded leather)
Hit Points 45 (8d8 + 15)
Speed 30 ft.

STR	DEX	CON	INT	WIS	CHA
15 (+2)	15 (+2)	14 (+2)	14 (+2)	11 (+0)	14 (+2)

Saving Throws Str +4, Dex +4, Wis +2
Skills Deception +4, Survival +2
Senses passive Perception 10
Languages any two languages
Challenge 1 (200 XP)

ACTIONS

Multiattack. The rogue makes three melee attacks: two with its scimitar and one with its dagger. Or the rogue makes two ranged attacks with its daggers.

Scimitar. *Melee Weapon Attack:* +5 to hit, reach 5 ft., one target. *Hit:* 6 (1d6 + 3) slashing damage.

Dagger. *Melee or Ranged Weapon Attack:* +5 to hit, reach 5 ft. or range 20/60 ft., one target. *Hit:* 5 (1d4 + 3) piercing damage.

REACTIONS

Parry. The rogue adds 2 to its AC against one melee attack that would hit it. To do so, the rogue must see the attacker and be wielding a melee weapon.

Thrakos

Thrakos are a hybrid dragon that are unique to *Legendaria*. Although they do not grow as large as a typical green dragon, they are fearsome in their attacks. They are extremely rare, but relatively capable of planning their attacks on a party carefully—often stormy weather and under the cover of darkness.

THRAKOS
Huge monstrosity (dragon), Neutral Evil

Armor Class 17 (natural armor)
Hit Points 169 (16d12+64)
Speed 50 ft., climb 40 ft., swim 20 ft.

STR	DEX	CON	INT	WIS	CHA
23 (+6)	16 (+3)	18 (+4)	7 (-2)	14 (+2)	12 (+1)

Skills Perception +6, Stealth +7
Damage Immunities lightning
Senses darkvision 90 ft., passive Perception 16
Languages Draconic
Challenge 11 (7,200 XP)

ACTIONS

Multiattack. 2 attacks: one bite, and one to constrict.

Bite. +10 to hit, 5' reach; Hit: 22 (3d10+6) piercing.

Constrict. +10 to hit, 5' reach;17 (2d10+6) bludgeoning plus 17 (2d10+6) slashing. Target is grappled. DC 16 to escape.

Lightening Breath (Recharge 5-6). Exhales a line of lightening 20' long and 5' wide. DC 16 Dexterity save, taking 66 HP (12d10) lightening damage, or half as much on success.

Swallow. If grappled, bite attack results in target being swallowed. Target is blind and restrained and takes 21 (6d6) acid damage at the beginning of every turn. If Thrakos takes 30 HP damage or more on a single turn, it must succeed on a DC 14 Constitution save or regurgitate the target.

Tôlbanaki - Priest

A generally peaceful people, the **Tôlbanaki** are almost always found near swamps and tidal waters. Extremely rare, they tend to keep to themselves, though they are welcoming to those that approach them. While the source of their powers is unknown, the Tôlbanaki are especially known for their healing.

An homage to Tôlba, a legendary turtle who carried the world up from the depths of the ocean after Moskwas the muskrat dove down and gathered the mud to create the land. The myth is from the Abenaki, indigenous to North America. (Courtesy of Jessa)

TOLBANAKI
Medium elemental, lawful

Armor Class 11 (natural armor)
Hit Points 110 (13d8 + 52)
Speed 40 ft.

STR	DEX	CON	INT	WIS	CHA
12 (+1)	10 (+0)	18 (+4)	12 (+1)	16 (+3)	14 (+2)

Saving Throws Con +7
Skills Insight +6, Perception +6
Damage Immunities bludgeoning, piercing, and slashing from nonmagical weapons
Condition Immunities incapacitated, paralyzed, petrified
Senses darkvision 30 ft., passive Perception 16
Languages Common
Challenge 5 (1,800 XP)

Limited Magic Immunity. The tolbanaki can't be affected or detected by spells of 2nd level or lower unless it wishes to be. It has advantage on saving throws against all other spells and magical effects.

Innate Spellcasting. The tolbanaki's innate spellcasting ability is Charisma (spell save DC 13, +5 to hit with spell attacks). The tolbanaki can innately cast the following spells, requiring no material components:

At will: mending, resistance, spare the dying
3/day each: cure wounds, protection from evil, remove curse
1/day: mass cure wounds

ACTIONS

Multiattack. The tolbanaki makes two claw attacks

Claw. +7 to hit, 5' reach; Hit: 9 (2d6 + 2) slashing.

Name: Jessa

Tôlbanaki - Warrior

The **Tôlbanaki** are a peaceful tribe of humanoids, so warriors are a small, rare number amongst them. However, they are formidable foe as their shells and scaly skin afford them strong defense, and their very nature means that, even as warriors, they know a limited number of healing and magical spells as well. It would be exceptional for the Tôlbanaki to do anything more than defend themselves, though there is a chance that they might join a party in limited numbers if their goals were aligned in a common fashion.

TOLBANAKI - WARRIOR
Medium elemental, lawful

Armor Class 16 (natural armor)
Hit Points 110 (13d8 + 52)
Speed 40 ft., burrow 5 ft., swim 10 ft.

STR	DEX	CON	INT	WIS	CHA
16 (+3)	10 (+0)	18 (+4)	12 (+1)	16 (+3)	14 (+2)

Saving Throws Str +6, Con +7
Skills Athletics +6, Survival +6
Damage Immunities bludgeoning, piercing, and slashing from nonmagical weapons
Condition Immunities incapacitated, paralyzed, petrified
Senses darkvision 30 ft., passive Perception 13
Languages Common
Challenge 5 (1,800 XP)

Limited Magic Immunity. The tolbanaki - warrior can't be affected or detected by spells of 2nd level or lower unless it wishes to be. It has advantage on saving throws against all other spells and magical effects.

Innate Spellcasting. The tolbanaki - warrior's innate spellcasting ability is Charisma (spell save DC 13, +5 to hit with spell attacks). The tolbanaki - warrior can innately cast the following spells, requiring no material components:

At will: disguise self
2/day each: charm person, cure light wounds

ACTIONS

Multiattack. The tolbanaki - warrior makes two claw attacks

Claw. +9 to hit, 5' reach; Hit: 12 (2d6 + 5) slashing.

Staff. +9 to hit, 5' reach; Hit: 18 (3d6)+6 bludgeoning.

Vance, Lord and Lady

Lord and Lady Vance are an unusual couple of fighters who are resistant to magic, but who rely heavily on attacks from wind and lightning. The party may be attacked by them during a storm if they are near a Keep or Castle that the Lord and Lady call home.

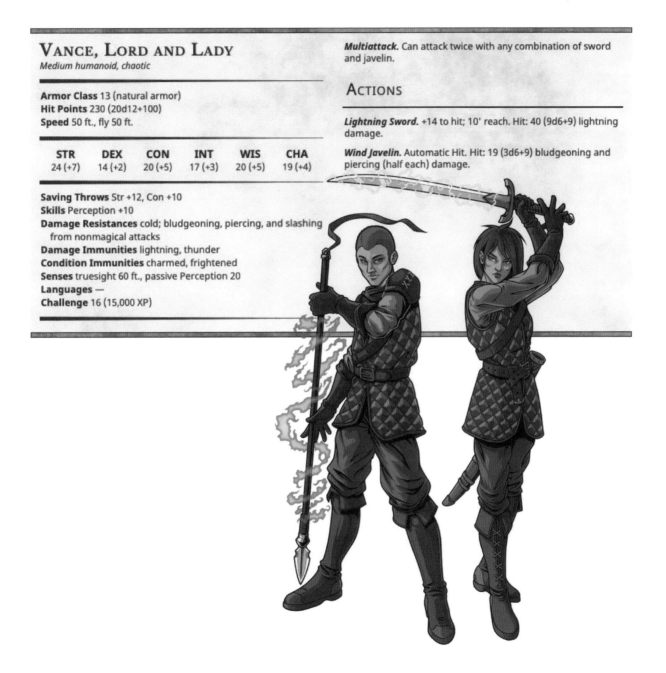

VANCE, LORD AND LADY
Medium humanoid, chaotic

Armor Class 13 (natural armor)
Hit Points 230 (20d12+100)
Speed 50 ft., fly 50 ft.

STR	DEX	CON	INT	WIS	CHA
24 (+7)	14 (+2)	20 (+5)	17 (+3)	20 (+5)	19 (+4)

Saving Throws Str +12, Con +10
Skills Perception +10
Damage Resistances cold; bludgeoning, piercing, and slashing from nonmagical attacks
Damage Immunities lightning, thunder
Condition Immunities charmed, frightened
Senses truesight 60 ft., passive Perception 20
Languages —
Challenge 16 (15,000 XP)

Multiattack. Can attack twice with any combination of sword and javelin.

ACTIONS

Lightning Sword. +14 to hit; 10' reach. Hit: 40 (9d6+9) lightning damage.

Wind Javelin. Automatic Hit. Hit: 19 (3d6+9) bludgeoning and piercing (half each) damage.

Undead (Vathris)

Vathris was originally used as an NPC that set the party off on a quest on his behalf. Although he will be manipulating the party (he is chaotic evil), it will be nearly impossible for the party to see through the deception. Vathris is quite manipulative and will tell the party there is great urgency for them to complete the quest (whatever that may be). Vathris will not accompany the party, but will reappear at the end of the quest.

VATHRIS
Medium humanoid, chaotic evil

Armor Class 17 (natural armor)
Hit Points 195 (26d8+78)
Speed 40 ft.

STR	DEX	CON	INT	WIS	CHA
15 (+2)	15 (+2)	17 (+3)	23 (+6)	21 (+5)	18 (+4)

Saving Throws Dex +7, Con +8, Wis +10
Skills Deception +9, Insight +10, Perception +10
Damage Resistances cold, fire, lightning
Condition Immunities charmed, exhaustion, frightened, poisoned
Senses truesight 60 ft., passive Perception 20
Languages —
Challenge 16 (15,000 XP)

Infernal Glare. vathris targets one party member within 60' who must succeed on a DC 17 Wisdom saving throw or become fright3ned of vathris for three turns (2/day).

Multiattack. Can attack twice with a great sword.

Healing. One creature vathris touches (or himself) regains up to 100 HP (1/day).

ACTIONS

Great Sword. +13, 5' reach; Hit: 20 (4d6+6) slashing plus 10 (3d6) acid damage.

REACTIONS

Resistance. If vathris fails a saving throw, he can elect to succeed (2/day).

Wiisagi-ma (Coyote)

Coyote is one of the *Sapelo Island* demigods. He is legendary for the tricks that he will play on unsuspecting parties. If he does attack, there will almost always be some element of trickery involved. He is a very careful foe and will retreat if he suspects defeat.

A FRIEND TO MAKWA. Wiisagi-ma is allied with **Makwa** and will come to his aid (teleportation) within two turns.

COYOTE
Large fey (Coyote), Chaotic Good

Armor Class 17 (natural armor)
Hit Points 175
Speed 50 ft., climb 40 ft.

STR	DEX	CON	INT	WIS	CHA
15 (+2)	22 (+6)	17 (+3)	16 (+3)	18 (+4)	21 (+5)

Saving Throws Str +7, Con +8, Wis +9
Skills Acrobatics +11, Deception +10, Perception +9, Stealth +11
Damage Resistances bludgeoning, piercing, and slashing from nonmagical attacks
Condition Immunities charmed, exhaustion, frightened, incapacitated, poisoned
Senses blindsight 30 ft., darkvision 120 ft., passive Perception 19
Languages All, telepathy 120 ft.
Challenge 13 (10,000 XP)

Legendary Resistance. (3/day) Can choose ot make a failed saving throw

Safe Fall. If coyote falls, he lands on his feet and takes no damage.

Shapechanger. Can morph into a human male, or coyote. Statistics are the same for either.

Innate Spellcasting. Spellcasting is Charisma (spell save DC 19) Can cast:
   At will: dispel magic, invisibility; 3/day each: counterspell, pass without trace; 1/day each: maze

Rejuvenation. If coyote dies, he reforms on the astral plane in 1d6 days.

ACTIONS

Multi-Attack. Makes two moon strike attacks in human form; in coyote form: two attacks with claws or one moon strike and one bite.

Bite. +11, reach 5'; Hit: 15 (2d8+6) piercing damage (coyote only)

Claw. +11, reach 5'; Hit: 13 (2d6+6) slashing damage plus 9 (2d8) radiant damage (coyote only)

Moon Strike. Spell Attack: +10 to hit, range 90', Hit: 22 (4d10) radiant damage. Succeed on DC18 dexterity or target glows and can't hide. Next attack against target then has advantage.

Keen Smell. Advantage on wisdom (perception) checks requiring smell

Magic Resistance. Advantage on all saving throws against spells and magic effects.

Pounce. If coyote can move 20' toward target, and hits with a clawed attack, target must succeed on DC 19 strength save or be knocked prone.

LEGENDARY ACTIONS

3 legendary Actions; can be used at any time; can re-use at beginning of turn Leap: Move up to speed, ignoring difficult terrain, if terrain is forest. Swipe: Makes a claw attack

Witch (Quespa)

Quespa is an undead witch, who is particularly deadly. Local lore has it that, out of unfounded revenge, she created the race of **Quesper**, or **Alligator people**. If the party encounters the Quesper, it is likely that they will ask for help in defeating the witch and freeing them from her deadly curse. If the party succeeds in defeating Quespa, they should be richly rewarded.

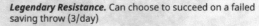

QUESPA
Medium undead (Human), Evil

Armor Class 18 (natural armor)
Hit Points 135 (18d8 + 54)
Speed 30 ft.

STR	DEX	CON	INT	WIS	CHA
11 (+0)	16 (+3)	16 (+3)	20 (+5)	14 (+2)	16 (+3)

Saving Throws Con +7, Int +9, Wis +6
Skills Arcana +13, History +13, Insight +6, Perception +6
Damage Resistances damage from spells; non magical bludgeoning, piercing, and slashing (from stoneskin)
Damage Immunities cold, lightning, necrotic
Condition Immunities charmed, exhaustion, frightened, paralyzed, poisoned
Senses passive Perception 16
Languages any six languages
Challenge 10 (5,900 XP)

Magic Resistance. The archmage has advantage on saving throws against spells and other magical effects.

Legendary Resistance. Can choose to succeed on a failed saving throw (3/day)

Rejuvination. Turn Resistance: Spell save DC 20 and +12 to hit with spell attacks; advantage on turn undead

Paralyzing Touch. +12 to hit, 10 (3d6) cold damage; save on DC 18 constitution or be paralyzed for 1 minute; can repeat save

ACTIONS

Spells. Cantrips (4): mage hand, prestidigitation, ray of frost

  1st level (4 slots): detect magic, magic missile, shield thunder wave
  2nd (3): detect thoughts, invisibility, Melf's acid arrow, mirror image
  3rd (3): animate dead, counterspell, dispell magic, fireball
  4th (3): blight, dimension door
  5th (3): cloudkill, scrying
  6th (1): disintegrate, globe of invulnerability
  7th (1): finger of death, plane shift
  8th (1): dominate monster, power word stun
  9th (1): power word kill

LEGENDARY ACTIONS

The High Priestess can take 3 legendary actions, choosing from the options below. Only one legendary action option can be used at a time and only at the end of another creature's turn. The archmage regains spent legendary actions at the start of its turn.

3 Legendary Actions. Cantrip: Casts a cantrip

  Paralyzing Touch: Uses Paralyzing Touch

  Frightening Gaze (costs 2 actions): Focuses gaze on one character who must make a DC 18 Wisdom save or become frightened for 1 minute. May repeat the saving throw at the end of each turn.

  Disrupt Life (costs 3 actions): Each character within 20' must make a DC 18 constitution save or take 21 (6d6) necrotic damage, or half as much on a successful save.

Yule Lads

In many respects, **Yule Lads** is a misnomer for a small band of troll-like creatures who inhabit forested areas. They are often seen traveling after sundown, riding upon large goats. They will attack and kill without mercy, though are cowardly at heart—and will retreat if they feel outnumbered.

YULE LADS

Medium fiend, chaotic evil

Armor Class 19 (natural armor)
Hit Points 82(11d10 + 21)
Speed 30 ft.

STR	DEX	CON	INT	WIS	CHA
19 (+4)	16 (+3)	16 (+3)	11 (+0)	12 (+1)	13 (+1)

Damage Resistances cold, fire; bludgeoning, piercing, and slashing from nonmagical attacks
Damage Immunities poison
Senses darkvision 120 ft., passive Perception 11
Languages Abyssal
Challenge 4 (1,100 XP)

Weakening Gaze. Targets one creature within 20'. Target must make DC 13 Constitution save. On fail, target's damage is cut in half for one minute. Target may repeat save at end of turns.

ACTIONS

Multiattack. The yule lads makes two melee attacks. May use weakening gaze befor or after these attacks.

Claw. *Melee Weapon Attack:* +6 to hit, reach 10 ft., one target. *Hit:* 11 (2d6 + 4) bludgeoning damage. The target is grappled (escape DC 14) if it is a Large or smaller creature and the chuul doesn't have two other creatures grappled.

Innate Spellcasting. Spellcasting: Wisdom, DC 11

May cast at will: darkness, dispel magic, fear, heat metal and levitate

Ziigwan-Miskwa (Stag)

The **Ziigwan-Miskwa** is a solitary hunter. She is held in the highest of esteems by the other *Legendaria* demi-gods and any of them will readily come to her aid when she requests. She is relentless in her hunt and will strike with precision and indifference. Her bow is her weapon of choice, and she will resist melee combat unless she is certain that it will lead to a successful hunt.

A FRIEND TO Morigann. Ziigwan-Miskwa is allied with **Morrigann** and will come to her aid (teleportation) within two turns.

ZIIGWAN-MISKWA
Medium fey, lawful neutral

Armor Class 21 (natural armor)
Hit Points 221 (27d8 + 100)
Speed 40 ft.

STR	DEX	CON	INT	WIS	CHA
19 (+4)	23 (+6)	20 (+5)	16 (+3)	17 (+3)	16 (+3)

Saving Throws Str +10, Wis +9, Cha +9
Skills Athletics +10, Perception +9, Survival +9
Damage Resistances acid, bludgeoning, piercing, slashing; bludgeoning, piercing, and slashing from nonmagical attacks
Damage Immunities poison
Condition Immunities charmed, exhaustion, frightened, poisoned
Senses blindsight 10 ft., darkvision 60 ft., passive Perception 19
Languages Common, Elvish, Sylvan
Challenge 18 (20,000 XP)

Legendary Resistance (3/day). If ziigwan-miskwa fails a saving throw, he can choose to succeed instead.

Magic Weapons. The Lord of the Hunt's weapon attacks are magical.

Spellcasting. ziigwan-miskwa's spell casting ability is Charisma (Save DC 16). She can cast the following spells:

At will: druidcraft, hunter's mark, phantom steed
3/day: commune with nature, conjure volley
1/day: summon fey (only the other Demigods of Legendaria, bear, badger, crow, coyote)

ACTIONS

Multiattack. ziigwan-miskwa makes three melee attacks or ranged attacks

Stalker's Spear. Melee or Ranged Weapon Attack: +8 to hit, 5' reach. or range 60/120 ft., one target. *Hit:* 12 (2d6 + 5) piercing damage or 14 (2d8 + 5) piercing damage if used in two hands, plus 7 (2d6) poison. If the target is a creature, it must succeed on a DC 19 Strength saving throw or be knocked prone. As a bonus action, ziigwan-miskwa can cause his spear to magically appear in her hand, even if it is destroyed.

Sharpshooters Longbow. Ranged Weapon Attack: +10 to hit, range 150/600 ft., one target. *Hit:* 13 (2d8 + 4) piercing damage plus 7 (2d6) poison damage.

REACTIONS

Parry. ziigwan-miskwa adds 6 to his AC against one attack that would hit her. She must see the attacker and must be wielding a melee weapon.

LEGENDARY ACTIONS

Ziigwan-Miskwa can take 3 legendary actions, choosing from the options below. Only one legendary action option can be used at a time and only at the end of another creature's turn. Ziigwan-Miskwa regains spent legendary actions at the start of his turn.

Strike. ziigwan-miskwa makes a stalker's spear attack or a sharpshooter's longbow attack.
Swift Stride. ziigwan-miskwa moves half his speed, or half the speed of any steed she rides.

Zormanth

Sailors from all walks of life tremble at the mention of **Zormanth**. Few have lived to tell of the deadly attacks by this terrifying denizen. Zormanth almost exclusively attacks in the middle of storms—causing many to believe it is only of myth and legend. It will relentlessly avoid attacking ships, instead focusing on those that struggle to keep it afloat. The Zormanth will attack with *psionic storm* from as far away as practical before it moves in and starts pulling sailors overboard into the dark depths. Zormanth will likely have a lair of treasure from ships it has plundered.

ZORMANTH

Large monstrosity, chaotic evil

Armor Class 12 (natural armor)
Hit Points 75 (10d8+30)
Speed 0 ft., swim 40 ft.

STR	DEX	CON	INT	WIS	CHA
12 (+1)	10 (+0)	16 (+3)	10 (+0)	15 (+2)	14 (+2)

Skills Perception +5
Damage Immunities bludgeoning, piercing, and slashing from nonmagical weapons
Senses truesight 120 ft., passive Perception 15
Languages —
Challenge 5 (1,800 XP)

ACTIONS

Multiattack. zormanth makes one tentacle attacks and one bite.

Bite. +7 to hit, 5' reach, Hit: 23 (3d8 + 10) piercing damage.

Tentacle. +7, 20' reach; Hit: 20 (3d6 + 10) bludgeoning damage, and the target is grappled (escape DC 18). Until this grapple ends, the target is restrained. zormanth may only grapple one target.

Psionic Storm. The zormanth magically creates three psionic bolts, each of which can strike a target the zormanth can see within 120 feet of it. A target must make a DC 18 Dexterity saving throw, taking 22 (4d10) psionic damage on a failed save, or half as much damage on a successful one.

Name: Richard Sorden

APPENDICES: NONPLAYER CHARACTERS

Abena (Paladin)

Human, Missionary, Neutral Good (Paladin); 3rd Level

Armor Class	18 (studded armor)	Initiative +2
Hit Points	55 (7 d10)	Proficiency +3
Speed	30'	

STR	DEX	CON	INT	WIS	CHA
17 (+3)	14 (+2)	14 (+2)	13 (+1)	12 (+1)	14 (+2)

Saving Throws	Wisdom +3, Charisma +4
Skills	Athletics +3, History +1, Insight +1, Persuasion +2
Senses	Passive Perception: 10
Languages	Common, Elvish, Goblin
Fight Style	Defense
Divine Smite	Extra 2d8 damage (costs spell slot)

Weapon	**ATK Bonus**	**Damage**
Longsword	+6	d10 + 4

Long Sword +1

Treasure: 0 cp   5 sp   0 ep   165 gp   0 pp

EQUIPMENT

Clothes	Signet Ring	Dice Set
Chain Shirt	Shield	Backpack
Bedroll	Rations (7)	

ACTIONS: Spellcasting

Spells:

Cantrips (3): Divine sense, Lay on hands
1st level (4 slots): Cure wounds, detect magic

Adena (Fighter)

Human, Neutral (Fighter); 1ˢᵗ Level

Armor Class	18 (chain armor)	Initiative +1	
Hit Points	14 (1d10)	Proficiency +2	
Speed	30'		

STR	DEX	CON	INT	WIS	CHA
16 (+3)	12 (+1)	19 (+4)	9 (-1)	10 ()	13 (+1)

Saving Throws	Strength +5, Constitution +6
Skills	Acrobatics +3, Intimidation +3
Senses	Passive Perception: 9
Languages	Common, Dwarvish
Fighting Style	Archer (+2)
Second Wind	1d10+Level

Weapon	ATK Bonus	Damage
Crossbow	+5	d8 + 3
Battle Axe	+5	d8 + 3

Treasure: 0 cp   0 sp   0 ep   0 gp   0 pp

Potion of Healing (2)

EQUIPMENT

Chain Mail	Shield	Backpack
Rations (6)	Torches (4)	Tinder
Bedroll	Rope	

Ander (Fighter)

Human, Fighter (Champion); 6th Level

Armor Class	16 (18) (chain mail)	Initiative +2
Hit Points	55 (6d10)	Proficiency +3
Speed	30'	

STR	DEX	CON	INT	WIS	CHA
18 (+4)	15 (+2)	17 (+3)	11 ()	9 (-1)	9 (-1)

Saving Throws	Strength +7, Constitution +6
Skills	Athletics +7, Perception +2, Stealth +5
Senses	Passive Perception: 9
Languages	Common, Goblin

Weapon	ATK Bonus	Damage
Crossbow, Light	+6	d8 + 4
Longsword	+6	d8 + 4 (or d10 if 2-handed)

Can attack twice
Fighting Style   Archery (+2)
Second wind (1d10+level)
Action surge

Potion of Healing (2)
Slippers of Spider Climbing

Treasure: 19 cp   31 sp   0 ep   62 gp   2 pp

EQUIPMENT

Rations (6)	Backpack	Bedroll	Clothing
Water Skin	Shovel	Lantern	Oil (3)
Iron Spikes (6)	Crowbar	Grappling Hook	
Horse	Horse Tack		

Berna (Cleric)

Level	3		**Cleric, Half Elf**	
Armor Class	18 (chain mail, shield)		**Initiative**	+0
Hit Points	28		**Proficiency**	+2
Speed	30'			

STR	DEX	CON	INT	WIS	CHA
14 (+2)	10 ()	16 (+3)	8 (-1)	16 (+3)	10 ()

Senses	Darkvision 30', passive Perception 13
Languages	Elf, orc, goblin, draconic, common

SKILLS

Insight +5, Medicine +5, Persuasion +2, Religion +1
Immune to magical sleep; advantage vs. charm

ACTIONS

Mace:	+4 to hit; 1d6 + 2 bludgeoning damage
Lt Crossbow:	+3 to hit; 1d8+1 piercing damage
Divine Smite: 1d8	on melee hit, can spend one spell slot to deal extra radiant damage, 1d8; add if target is undead or fiend
Divine Sense:	(4x/long rest): until the end of next turn, know location of any celestial, fiend or undead within 60'.
Lay Hands:	Point pool: Lvl + 5HP; Action: Heal any number of HP up to pool remaining; can cure one disease or poison for 5HP.
Divine Health:	Immune to disease
Cantrips:	Sacred Flame, resistance, spare the dying
1st Lvl Spells: (4 slots)	Bless, cure light wounds, detect magic, shield of faith, guiding bolt, command
2nd Lvl Spells: (2 slots)	Lesser restoration, spiritual weapon, hold person, prayer of healing

Treasure: 150 cp	0 sp	5 ep	57 gp	0 pp

EQUIPMENT

Chain Mail, Shield
Bolts (20), Light Crossbow
Backpack, blanket
Rations, Waterskin

Castor (Wizard)

Level	3	Wizard, Human (Necromancy)	
Armor Class	13	**Initiative**	+2
Hit Points	34	**Proficiency**	+2
Speed	30'		

STR	DEX	CON	INT	WIS	CHA
10 ()	14 (+2)	14 (+2)	16 (+3)	18 (+4)	14 (+2)

Senses — Passive Perception 13
Languages — Common, Elvish, Farfey, Draconish

SKILLS

Insight +5, Medicine +5, Persuasion +2, Religion +1
Immune to magical sleep; advantage vs. charm

ACTIONS

Dagger: +4 to hit; 1d4
Quarterstaff: +2 to hit; 1d6 (1d8)

Cantrips: Dancing lights, minor illusion, firebolt
1st Lvl Spells: Comprehend languages, detect magic, mage armor, magic missile,
(2 slots) Tasha's hideous laughter, unseen servant, hellish rebuke, shield
2nd Lvl Spells: Hold person, spider climb
(2 slots)

Treasure   0 cp   3 sp   0 ep   99 gp   0 pp

EQUIPMENT

Spellbook	Blank Ink	Quill
Small knife	Clothes	Horse (riding)
Horse Tack	Rations (7)	Rope

Ring of protection +1
Ioun Stone, widom +2

Chief Wapuka (Druid)

Chief Wapuka will be found in the forest by himself. He will tell the party that he is gathering herbs and plants for healing ceremonies. He will also share that he is fearful of whatever monster is haunting the part of the adventure where you would like Chief Wapuka to first appear, and he will gladly join the party if asked. As the adventure continues, Chief Wapuka will occasionally express frustration and wanting to find a way back to his village. However, the system of portals will offer him no opportunity but to try and conclude the quest in the hopes of finally finding his way back home.

Human, Scout/Shaman (Druid); 3rd Level

Armor Class	15 (leather)		Initiative	+2	
Hit Points	30 (3 d8 hit dice)		Proficiency	+2	
Speed	30'				

STR	DEX	CON	INT	WIS	CHA
14 (+2)	14 (+2)	16 (+3)	15 (+2)	18 (+4)	12 (+1)

Saving Throws	Int +4, Wis +6
Skills	Insight +6, Medicine +6, Religion +4, Survival +6
Senses	passive wisdom: 18
Languages	common, druidic, goblin, gnoll

Weapon	**ATK Bonus**	**Damage**
Quarterstaff	+4	1d6+2
Dart	+4	1d4+2

Leather armor (11)
Shield (+2)
Darts (10)

Can use **wild shape** as a bonus action

Spellcasting (save DC 14; +6 to hit with spell attacks)

ACTIONS

Spells:

Cantrips:	Thorn whip (1d6), resistance
1st:	Goodberry, speak with animals, animal friendship, charm person
2nd:	Darkvision, find traps

Erlon (Paladin)

Level	4		**Paladin, Half Elf**		
Armor Class	18 (chain mail, shield)		**Initiative**	+1	
Hit Points	38		**Proficiency**	+2	
Speed	30'				

STR	DEX	CON	INT	WIS	CHA
16 (+3)	12 (+1)	14 (+2)	8 (-1)	10 ()	16 (+3)

Saving Throws	Str +3, Dex +1 Con +2, Int -1, Wis +2, Cha +5
Senses	Darkvision 60', passive Perception 10
Languages	Elf, dwarf, goblin, common

SKILLS

Athletics +5, History +1, Insight +2, Intimidation +5, Medicine +2, Persuasion +5
Immune to magical sleep; advantage vs. charm

ACTIONS

Longsword:	+5 to hit; 1d8 + 3 slashing damage
Javelin:	+3 to hit; 1d6+1 piercing damage
Fighting Style:	+2 dmg if fighting with one melee weapon

Divine Smite:	on melee hit, can spend one spell slot to deal extra radiant damage, 1d8; add 1d8 if target is undead or fiend
Divine Sense:	(4x/long rest): until the end of next turn, know location of any celestial, fiend or undead within 60'.
Lay Hands:	Point pool: Lvl + 5HP; Action: Heal any number of HP up to pool remaining; can cure one disease or poison for 5HP.
Divine Health:	Immune to disease

1st Lvl Spells:	detect magic, heroism, protection from evil and good, shield of faith, bane, hunter's mark, bless

Gorgo(Wizard)

Level	2	**Wizard, Human (Necromancy)**	
Armor Class	12	**Initiative**	+0
Hit Points	18	**Proficiency**	+2
Speed	30'		

STR	DEX	CON	INT	WIS	CHA
12 (+1)	15 (+2)	16 (+3)	18 (+4)	14 (+2)	12 (+1)

Senses	Passive Perception 11
Languages	Common, Orc

SAVES & SKILLS

Intelligence +6, Wisdom +4
Insight +4, Investigation +6, Medicine +4, Religion +6
Arcane Recovery
Grim Harvest: regain HP by 2HP spell level. Doesn't work on undead

ACTIONS

Qtr Staff:	+3 to hit; 1d6 + 1 bludgeoning damage
Lt Crossbow:	+4 to hit; 1d8+2 piercing damage

Cantrips:	Acid splash, fire bolt, light
1st Lvl Spells:	Detect magic, find familiar, mage armor, magic missle, unseen
(2 slots)	servant, sleep

Treasure	0 cp	0 sp	0 ep	15 gp	0 pp

EQUIPMENT

Spell Book Torches (4) Shovel
Robe   Iron Spikes (10) Bedroll

Kura (Barbarian)

Level	1	**Barbarian (Human)**	
Armor Class	17 (chain mail, shield)	**Initiative**	+2
Hit Points	12	**Proficiency**	+2
Speed	30'		

STR	DEX	CON	INT	WIS	CHA
19 (+4)	14 (+2)	17 (+3)	13 (+1)	13 (+1)	10 ()

Senses   Passive Perception 13
Languages   Common, orc, goblin

SKILLS & SAVING THROWS

Strength +6, Constitution +5
Athletics +6, Intimidation +2, Perception +3, Persuasion +2, Survival +3

ACTIONS

Great Axe: +6 to hit; 1d12 + 4 bludgeoning damage
Hand Axe (2): +4 to hit; 1d6+2 piercing damage
Javelin (2): +4 to hit; 1d6+2 piercing damage

Savage Attack: On a crit, roll 1d again and add to damage (melee)
Rage: +2 DMG; Resistance to bludgeoning, piercing, slashing damage
             (Duration: 1 minute)

Treasure   0 cp   0 sp   0 ep   38 gp   0 pp

EQUIPMENT

Shield	Backpack	Bedroll
Mess kit	Tinderbox	Torches (10)
Rations (10)	Waterskin	Grappling hook
Rope (50')	Staff	Hunting Trap

René Menard (Cleric)

Human, Missionary (Cleric); 6th Level

Armor Class	20 (studded leather)		Initiative	+10	
Hit Points	55 (7 d10 hit dice)		Proficiency	+3	
Speed	30'				

STR	DEX	CON	INT	WIS	CHA
12 (0)	20 (+5)	14 (+1)	14 (+2)	14 (+2)	9 (-1)

Saving Throws	Str +3, Dexterity +8
Skills	Animal Handling +5, Nature +5, Perception +5, Sleight of Hand +8,
	Stealth +8, Survival +5
Senses	passive wisdom: 12
Languages	common, elvish, goblin, orc
Favored Terrain	Forest
Favored Enemies	Humanoids, +2

Weapon	**ATK Bonus**	**Damage**	
Crossbow	+10	d8+7	
Longsword	+9	d8+5	(or d10 if 2-handed)
Shortsword	+9	d6+5	

Fighting Style	Archery
Hunter's Prey:	Horde Breaker (make 2nd attack on another creature within 5' of prev. target)

Boots of Elvenkind	Silence, advantage on stealth saves
Ring of Protection +1	+1 on all saving throws

Spellcasting (save DC 12; +4 to hit with spell attacks)

ACTIONS

Spells:

Cantrips: Minor Illusion

1st level (4 slots): Hail of thorns, goodberry, cure wounds, hunter's mark

2nd level (3 slots): Silence, find traps

Telchur (Wizard)

Level	2		**Wizard, Half-Elf**	
Armor Class	12		**Initiative**	+2
Hit Points	16		**Proficiency**	+2
Speed	30'			

STR	DEX	CON	INT	WIS	CHA
9 (-1)	14 (+2)	15 (+2)	18 (+4)	8 (-1)	13 (+1)

Senses	Darkvision 60', passive Perception 9
Languages	Common, orc, elvish, draconish, goblin

SKILLS & SAVING THROWS

Intelligence +6, Wisdom +1
Arcana +3, History +3, Investigation +6, Religion +6, Stealth +2
Advantage against magical sleep

Arcane Recovery: Recover ½ spell slots after short rest (1/day)

ACTIONS

Dagger (2):	+4 to hit; 1d4 + 2 piercing damage
Lt Crossbow:	+4 to hit; 1d8+1 piercing damage

Cantrips:	Mage hand, fire bolt, ray of frost
1ˢᵗ Lvl Spells:	Burning hands, charm person, feather fall, mage armor, magic missile,
(3 slots)	sleep

Treasure	8 cp	1 sp	0 ep	0 gp	0 pp

EQUIPMENT

Bolts	Component Pouch
Tinder Box	Rations (10)
Water Skin	Mess Kit

Velnius (Ranger)

Level	4	**Ranger, High Elf**	
Armor Class	19 (studded leather, shield)	**Initiative**	+10
Hit Points	55	**Proficiency**	+2
Speed	30'		

STR	DEX	CON	INT	WIS	CHA
11 ()	20 (+5)	13 (+1)	14 (+2)	14 (+2)	9 (-1)

Senses	Darkvision 90', passive Perception 12
Languages	Common, elvish, goblin, orc, giant

SKILLS

Animal Handling +5, Nature +5, Perception +5, Sleight of Hand +8, Stealth +8., Survival +5
Immune to magical sleep; advantage vs. charm
Primeval Awareness: sense creatures

Favored enemies: Humanoids (+4 damage)
Greater favored enemies: Giants (+4 damage)

Hunter's Prey: Hord Breaker (2nd attack on another target witin 5' of previous target)
Feat: Alert; cannot be surprised; +5 initiative

ACTIONS

Crossbow:	+10 to hit; 1d8 + 7 piercing damage
Longsword*:	+8 to hit; 1d8 + 5 slashing damage
Shortsword:	+4 to hit; 1d6 + 5 slashing damage

* or d10 if two handed

1st Lvl Spells: (4 slots)	Goodberry (10), cure wounds, hunter's mark
2nd Lvl Spells: (3 slots)	Silence, find traps

EQUIPMENT

Studded leather, shield
Crossbow, Longsword, Short sword
Backpack, bedroll, waterskin
Rations (10 days)

APPENDICES: MORRIGAN'S LODGE OF LEGENDARY HUNTS

Overview: This is Morrigan's *Lodge of Legendary Hunts*: a place where the undead elven archer demigod transports her prey for the deadliest of hunts: their final. The main hunt area is **19-25**, and **25 (A-I)** are kennels for demon hounds that get released once per turn on their prey.

While the DM may design an encounter where the party enters through the front door, they may also be teleported to **(1)**, the teleport designated in the southwestern corner of **(18)** or directly to the hunt area **(19)**. Particularly strong parties may be teleported to **(1)** in the hopes of further weakening them as they explore the trophy rooms **(6-17)**. At any time, they may also be received by Morrigan in her chambers **(18)** before being released into the trophy rooms **or** directly to the hunt area **(19)**.

The Lodge – From the outside, the lodge appears to be little more than a hunting shack as only areas **(1)** and **(2)** are above ground and are roughly 20' x 30'in area. The exterior is in a location obscured by woods that are so dense that the forest never seems brighter than it would at dusk. When the party encounters it, they will have to be within at least 15' of it. The issue is dense foliage and ground cover, so additional light or darkvision will not improve the party's ability to see the lodge any sooner.

The lodge is constructed of wood from the surrounding trees. The exterior is dark, wet and rotting, though it appears to be solidly constructed. There is a door that is closed but unlocked. There are no windows. If the party looks, there is a chimney, but no smoke. There are wooden pillars on both sides of the door. They are modest but still betray the fact that the shack might be grander than it appears on the exterior. If the party inspects the pillars, they are all carved with horrifying visages of hunt and torture scenes. Whoever carved them appears to have not only relished the hunt, but of slowly and painfully torturing their prey. Worse: most of the prey is humanoid.

1. **Grand Entry:** The entry is exterior space, flanked by a narrow, but immensely long porch that extends to both the east and the west. Other than the double-doors the entry in unremarkable, but for its sheer size—again suggesting that this structure is more than a modest hunting shack.

   The doors are of wooden construction and are adorned with the same scenes as the pillars that surround the entry. They are unlocked and un-trapped. If the party inquires, both of those facts will strike them as mildly curious, though perhaps not alarming.

2. **Fountain:** A large fountain dominates the space in front of the double-doors that lead to the stairs **(3)**. It is an immense structure that is also of wooden construction. The water looks murky and foul, as though the fountain has not been maintained in quite some time. The room is unlit. There is no evidence that anyone has been in this room for an extremely long time, though it is also oddly devoid of any dust or cobwebs. Ask the party to make **Perception (or lore) DC 18** checks; regardless of the roll, they will not notice anything unusual in this space. However, they will feel a sense that everything in the lodge is meant as a trophy of some sort and they will have a relentless desire to explore the lodge regardless of the outcome. Party members that fail their save will not be deterred from their search and will fend off party members who try to stop them. They can remake their check every other time they inspect a trophy room.

The descriptions and rolls are designed to help you, as the DM, build a level of anxiety about the structure.

3. **Stairs (Down):** The main stairway drops 20' or so below the outside surface. They are also wooden, wet and extremely slippery. The stairwell is unlit. The players should be asked to roll a **DC 14 Dexterity** save or slip and fall. At the DM's discretion, they could take up to 1d4 damage from their falls, but the goal is to continue to build a sense of dread as the party progresses further into the lodge.

4. **West Hallway:** The only feature in the hallway is a secret door on the southern wall, in roughly the center of the hallway. Characters searching for secret doors will require only a **DC 6 Perception (Wisdom)** check to find an inset stone in the shape of a stag's head. If they place their hand in the shape, the secret door will open. There will be an obvious trap in the shape that can be found with a second **DC 6 Perception (Wisdom)** check as the goal should be a combination of foreboding but a false sense of security to go along with it.

5. **East Hallway:** The secret door and trap in the east hallway are identical to those in the **West Hallway (4)**.

6. **Trophy Room: DC 12 strength save,** *-1 strength*. The walls are adorned with the head and shoulder mounts of trophy animals. The fresh remains of the most recent trophy lie in the middle of the floor; its very presence weakens the knees of those who view it and fail their save.

7. **Trophy Room: DC 12 constitution save,** *-1 constitution*. This looks like a future trophy room being used for the visceral remains of trophies as they are being taxidermied. The combination of the smell and visual, are impossible to ignore.

8. **Trophy Room: DC 12 dexterity save,** *-1 dexterity*. The trophy walls look more like a neglected dungeon as there are kobold corpses hung from every wall, and the floors are slick with gore. Slipping and falling will cause lasting soreness and limit mobility.

9. **Trophy Room: DC 12 perception save (wisdom),** *-1 disadvantage on savings throws*. All of the trophies in this room were once majestic birds. Glancing at the trophies, and their eyes in particular, will trigger the saving throws. Magically, all of the eyes in these trophies give the impression that the birds are still alive.

10. **Trophy Room: DC 12 constitution save,** *-10 HP*. This trophy features what were impressively large and strong beasts. They are all extremely intimidating in size and stature. Their very presence can have the impact of making the party going temporarily weak in the knees.

11. **Trophy Room: DC 12 dexterity save,** *disadvantage on ranged weapon attacks*. The saving throw should be made once a party member has stepped 5' into the room and will impact all party members in the room. There are pressure plates on the room that are indiscernible, but the save reflects a party members' ability to dodge a number of trophies that drop from a false ceiling and swing wildly. A failure means

that a party member has been hit multiple times by trophies and will take some time to recover from the trauma.

12. **Trophy Room: DC 12 strength save,** *disadvantage on melee attacks*. This room functions in the same fashion as **(11)**, but the effect is different in that the trauma will cause a temporary reduction in strength as it applies to melee attacks.

13. **Trophy Room: DC 12 wisdom save,** *-2 spell attacks*. The sheer terror of the trophy rooms starts to take its toll on the party. While there is nothing very different about this room, those who fail this saving throw are starting to feel the full effects of the sheer depravity of the trophy rooms in the lodge.

14. **Trophy Room: DC 12 constitution save,** *-1 constitution*. Even from the doorway, this room is remarkably empty; however, as soon as the party enters, a foul stench starts to emanate from the walls near the floor. A failed save causes the party member to vomit.

15. **Trophy Room: DC 12 strength save,** *-1 strength*. This room is identical to **(12)**.

16. **Trophy Room: DC 12 dexterity save,** *-10' movement*. The floors of this trophy room are covered with gore. Any party member who steps foot into the room makes a saving throw or will injure themselves enough to restrain their movement while they recover.

17. **Trophy Room: DC 12 dexterity save,** *-10' movement*. This room is identical to **(16)**.

18. **Main Chamber:** Morrigan's main chambers. The chamber includes teleportation to the hunt and observation deck (north eastern corner) and in/out of the chamber (south western corner). The teleportation site into 18 is located at **17**.

19. **Hunt Chamber, Main Grounds:** The main hunting grounds are larger than they appear. Assume each square is 20'. There are a number of features described below that the party might choose to use to either their advantage or disadvantage as the hounds are released.

20. **Lake:** The 5' deep corner of the lake is home to a swarm of **x**, the 10' corner to a small **y**, and the 40' center to a **z**. If the party is attacked by either **x** or **y**, the other will also swim to the attack, joining the fight at the start of their initiative in the second turn. The lake is too shallow for **z** to leave the deepest part of the lake.

21. **Cabin:** This is a small, windowless cabin in the northwestern corner of the hunting grounds. The door to the cabin is missing. If the party enters the cabin, the demon dogs will retreat into the forest and have partial cover while they wait. After two turns, Morrigan will use her bow to start the cabin on fire. The party will have two additional turns to leave without smoke or fire damage. For every turn they remain, they will take 1d8 damage.

22. **Woods:** The woods and swamp **(23)** probably provide the best opportunities for the party to survive as both will give them partial cover. There are platinum eagles **(2)** that inhabit the eastern side of the woods near the kennel. They cannot attack the

party while they are in the woods, but will attack elsewhere on the hunting grounds, exclusively from the air.

23. Swamp: The swamp is extremely wet and difficult to traverse, cutting speed in half, and melee attacks occurring at disadvantage. There are alligator people **(4)** located in the swamp on the northeast corner of the lake **(20)**. Although they will attack when the party enters the swamp, they will not pursue outside of the swamp.

24. Observation Deck: Morrigan will initially observe the hunt from a luxurious observation deck. The observation deck is visible from the southern shores of the lake and river that bisect the hunting grounds. It is surrounded by a wrought iron fence that is only scalable with a **DC 18 Acrobatics (Dexterity)** save as it is both very tall and slippery. Players making the attempt must make the save twice, including at the top of the fence. A second failure results in 1d6 damage from the fall. They have a 50% chance of falling inside the observation deck area.

The Observation Deck is also accessible through a secret door on the south eastern side. The door involves pulling on one of the stakes in the fence and requires a **DC 16 perception (Wisdom)** check.

Although luxurious, there is nothing of value on the observation deck.

If Morrigan has not joined the hunt, she will defend herself while attempting to lure the party back onto the main hunt ground so that her demon hounds may aid in the hunt.

25. Demon Hound Kennels: A collection of 9 kennels, the doors will be opened, one for every turn of the hunt until all 9 demon hounds have been released.

A-I: Individual Demon Hound Kennels: Each kennel contains one demon hound. They otherwise contain nothing of value.

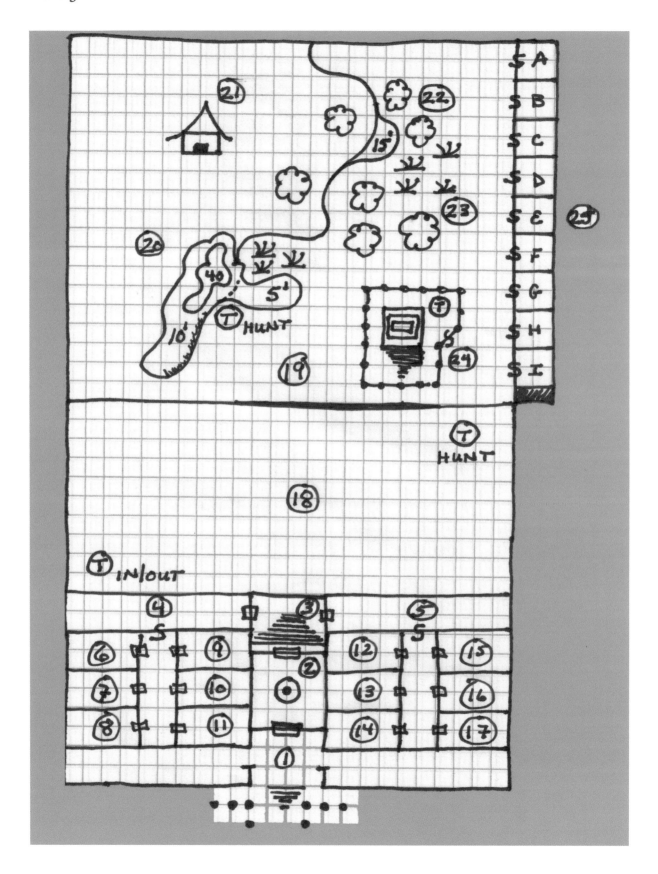

APPENDICES: MISAKAKOJIS'S DEADLY WARREN

Misakakojis will have one **legendary action** to teleport all creatures within a 30' radius to its *warren*. Affected creatures make a **DC 18 wisdom** save or will be teleported to separate locations based on a **D12**. Once they fail, they will teleport to a new location (**D12**) every turn.

At the start of every turn, characters make an additional **DC wisdom** save where the base save is **DC 18 – [number of successful saves]** or they will be teleported to a new (**DC12**) location. All of the locations are identical except for **10, 11 & 12** which will be the character's only hint that they are teleporting.

Misakakojis will remain at position (**D12**) and immediately attack any character that teleports to that location.

If a character looks for a secret door (**S**), they must make a **DC 18 perception (wisdom)** check. Once successful, the character gains a **+1 for every secret door they discover. Example:** If a character has saved **4 times** and found **2 secret doors**, they would make a **DC 14 wisdom save** against teleportation and **DC 16 perception check** to search for secret doors.

Each of the small rooms can hold up to three creatures or they (not **Misakakojis**) become prone and unable to attack. The large rooms can hold up to six creatures or they become prone.

Use the following table to keep track of character positions. **Circle secret doors** on the map that have been discovered.

Location A: Misakojis treasure warren. As a legendary creature, treasure should be significant.

	Room at Turn:											
Player	1	2	3	4	5	6	7	8	9	10	11	12
Misakakojis												

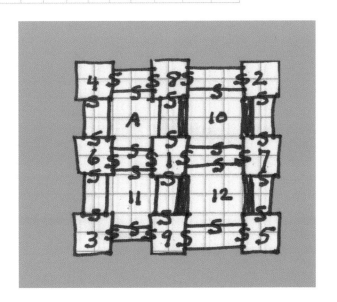

APPENDICES: CREATURES BY TYPE

BEAST

Badger, Large 9
Eagle, Platinum 24
Krake 37

DRAGON

Chirogon..16
Hodag 35
Thrakos 52

ELEMENTAL

Efreeti 26
Earth Elemental.......................................25

FEY

Chogan (Crow) 17
Makwa (Bear) 42
Misakokojish (Badger) 45
Morrigan, Elven Archer 46
Wiisagi-ma (Coyote) 57
Ziigwan-Miskwa (Stag) 60

FIEND

Ban Sith 10
Beast of Brey Road 11
Belsnickel (Demon)..................................12
Dartford Demon (Demon) 19
Demon 20
Demon, Dog...21
Demon, Vimak 22
Frau Perchta 27
Grýla..32
Hans Trapp 33
Jòlakötturinn..36
Krampus (Demon).....................................38
Père Fuettard 47

Yule Lads...59

HUMANOID

Assassin (Arsama) 7
Assassin (Korag) 8
Dwarf, Darkstone 23
Haunchies of Muskego 34
Quesper – Cleric 48
Quesper – Mage......................................49
Quesper – Warrior 50
Rogue 51
Tôlbanaki, Priest 53
Tôlbanaki, Warrior 54

MONSTROSITY

Bon Secour 13
Bulette 14
Catoblepis 15
Chozech 18
Gruagach..31
Lake Monster, Pepie.................................39
Lake Winnebago Monster 40
Mashenomak 43
Minotaur 44
Zormanth 61

UNDEAD

Abhartach..5
Arch Mage Bredon.....................................6
Ghost, Graceland 28
Ghost, Headless 29
Ghost, Ridgeway 30
Lich, Keraptis 41
Vance 55
Vathris 56
Witch, Quespa 58

APPENDICES: CREATURES BY CHALLENGE

CHALLENGE 1
Badger 9
Haunchies of Muskego 34
Krake 37
Rogue 51

CHALLENGE 3
Beast of Brey Road 11
Gruagach..31
Minotaur 44

CHALLENGE 4
Ban Sith 10
Chozech 18
Dwarf, Darkstone 23
Eagle, Platinum 24
Ghost, Ridgeway 30
Quesper 48
Yule Lads..59

CHALLENGE 5
Bulette..14
Catoblepas 15
Demon, Dartford 19
Earth Elemental.................................25
Grýla...32
Mashenomak 43
Tôlbanaki (Priest) 53
Tôlbanaki (Warrior) 54
Zormanth 61

CHALLENGE 6
Demon...20
Demon, Dog.......................................21
Hans Trapp 33

CHALLENGE 7
Chirogon...16
Frau Perchta.......................................27
Ghost, Headless 29
Père Fouettard...................................47

CHALLENGE 8
Assassin (Arsama) 7
Assassin (Korag) 8
Jòlakötturinn......................................36

CHALLENGE 9
Morrigan (Elven Archer)...........................46
Belsnickel 12

CHALLENGE 10
Witch (Quespa) 58

CHALLENGE 11
Bon Secour 13
Efreeti...26
Ghost, Graceland 28
Hodag...35
Thrakos...52

CHALLENGE 12
Arch Mage – Bredon...........................6

CHALLENGE 13
Abhartach..5
Wiisagi-ma (Coyote) 57

CHALLENGE 14
Chogan (Crow) 17
Lake Monster, Pepie.........................39

CHALLENGE 16
Demon, Vimak 22
Vance 55
Vathris 56

CHALLENGE 18
Ziigwan-Miskwa (Stag) 60

CHALLENGE 19
Krampus..38

CHALLENGE 21
Lich, Keraptis 41

CHALLENGE 22
Makwa (Bear) 42

CHALLENGE 23
Lake Winnebago Monster 40

CHALLENGE 25
Misakokojish (Badger) 45

ANY

Demon, Dartford 19
Demon 20
Demon, Dog 21
Jòlakötturinn 36
Rogue 51
Yule Lads 59

FOREST

Badger 9
Frau Perchta 27
Gruagach 31
Makwa (Bear) 42
Misakokojish (Badger) 45
Ziigwan-Miskwa (Stag) 60

GRASSLAND

Beast of Brey Road 11
Catoblepas 15
Chogan (Crow) 17
Ghost, Ridgeway 30
Grýla 32
Krake 37
Morrigan, Elven Archer 46

HILLS

Bulette 14
Earth Elemental 25
Haunchies of Muskego 34
Hodag 35
Wiisagi-ma (Coyote) 57

MOUNTAINS

Chirogon 16
Eagle, Platinum 24
Thrakos 52

SWAMP

Quesper - Cleric 48
Quesper – Mage 49
Quesper – Warrior 50
Tôlbanaki – Priest 53
Tôlbanaki – Warrior 54

UNDERGROUND

Abhartach 5
Arch Mage Bredon 6
Ban Sith 10
Demon, Vimak 22
Dwarf, Darkstone 23
Efreeti 26
Ghost, Graceland 28
Ghost, Headless 29
Lich, Keraptis 41
Minotaur 44
Vance 55
Vathris 56
Witch (Quespa) 58

UNDERWATER

Bon Secour 13
Chozech 18
Lake Monster, Pepie 39
Lake Winnebago Monster 40
Mashenomak 43
Zormanth 61

URBAN

Assassin (Arsama) 7
Assassin (Korag) 8
Belsnickel 12
Hans Trapp 33
Krampus 38
Père Fouttard 47

Axe of the Darkstone Dwarves – Usage: 1/day: Duration: 30 minutes. The bearer of the axe can detect precious metals within 15'. Other ability: +1 hand axe, mithril.

Conch of the Tôlbanaki – Usage: 1/day; Duration: 30 minutes. When the conch is blown near water, the deep, resonant sound will summon one of the following familiars. The familiar will fight with the party until its HP drops to 0 or lower, at which point it will simply disappear. Other ability: cannot be charmed or put to sleep by magical means.

Lantern of the Quesper – Usage: 1/day; Duration: 30 minutes. When the lantern is lit, it will summon 1d4 familiars. The familiars will fight with the party until its HP drops to 0 or lower, at which point it will simply disappear. The familiars could include: alligator, constrictor snake, giant rat or stirge.

Ring of Bredon – This ring is both a blessing and a curse. It is made of mithril and grants the wearer the ability to go undetected by undead creatures, giving them a disadvantage on **perception** checks to discover the wearer's location. Up to 1d6 lesser undead can follow the wearer's commands, per day. However, the wearer has 2 days to remove the ring or your skin will turn ashen grey and your **charisma** will be permanently reduced by 2. If the ring is removed, the wearer's skin will return to its normal color slowly over the period of 2 months; the **charisma** reduction is permanent unless cured by magical means.

Robe of the Platinum Eagles – Usage: 1/day: Duration: 1 hour. The wearer, through images and intuition, can communicate with any sentient being. Other ability: +1 protection.

Quespa's Book of Arcana – This book requires intensive study over 72 hours and a period of 6 days. The reader's Intelligence and Wisdom will both increase by 1, as does your maximum for each of those scores. The reader will have the ability to transform one humanoid race into a hybrid race with a small to medium beast of their choice (e.g. a bear or badger). The book loses its magic but regenerates it in 25 years.

APPENDIX: LEGENDARIA

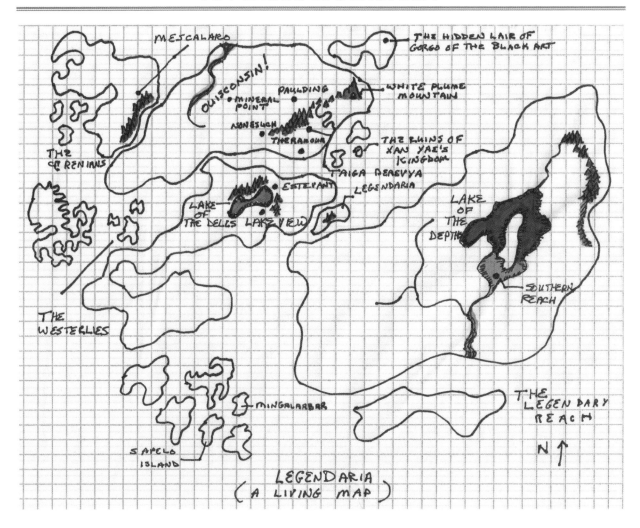

LEGENDARIA
(A LIVING MAP)

OPEN GAME LICENSE VERSION 1.0A

$2,625 Pledged (175%)
124 Supporters
December 2019

Kevin Watson
Chris Anderson
Robert Sabatke Jr
James Arnold
Stephen Gossman
Samantha Michaels
Tom Magness
Scott J. Dahlgren
Jangus C. Cooper
Tom Dodson
Olaf
John Bookwalter Jr.
The Creative Fund
Jeremiah Bruce
Trevor Hardy
Stephane Gelgoot
Kyle
Larry Edwards
Verllamica
Steven Beverage
Hayderino
Randy Smith
Timothy H.
Heath Dobson
Chris Berger
Yordi Schaeken
Ingvald Arne Meland
Howard Bampton
Samuel F.
Patrice Demagny
Vesala
Mark James Featherstone
Mike
Alex Wood
Raymond Fowkes Jr.
Philip Hindley
Ross Snyder
Chad Johnson
Lee Smith

Christian Cooper
Shane Nowak
Adam Bakow
Dan Friel
KickSME
Frank Tilley
Steven Daly
Luke Church
Stewart Hiskey
Neil
Benjamin P. Powell
Brian Tabares
Paul Logasa Bogen II
David Wenzel
Raymond E. Strawn III
Sophia
John Bowlin
Ryan
Basil Shepherd
Castreek
Alex Carman
S P
Byron
Daniel Steylemans
Thomas J Mahaney II
Saamy
Joshua Barry
DSH
Thomas Talamini
Ben
Michael Bakker
Christina Norr
Kyle James
Mary Zawacki
Andreas Loeckher
Trejaan Cavelion
Søren Dalsberg
Walmsey Family
Jason Hennigan
Pawel
SH Tan
Charlie Bijmans
Stephen E. Dinehart IV

Dana
Heather
Ashley Booker
Aranda Ray
Kevin McDonnell
Russell Ventigeglia
Sam Bateman
Erin Zeddies
Bailey Martin
Gilles Haun
Stacy
Lukefabis
Kiersty
Alec Hunter
Nickolas Szilagyi
Ryan James
Serena Kaye
Jason Gabel
Jon Terry
James Dillard
Scott Were
William Bossier
Norman White
Beckett Barnhisel
Nathaniel Guenther
Shaun Beckett
Liam Duffy
William Jones
Rob Fowler
Bethany Plank
Shawn McNaughton
M G
Maxime Bombardier
Kaitlin
Zerberoo
Gerald Englehart
Kevin Obrien

Contributors in **bold** also contributed names of monsters as part of the Kickstarter campaign.

MONSTER SKETCH BOOK

Sketch

magic
spell

Printed in Great Britain
by Amazon